P9-CFS-827

BUILDING A MYSTERY

You are so there.

TWITCHES

T·WITCHES

H.B. GILMOUR
& RANDI REISFELD

SCHOLASTIC

NEW YORK   TORONTO   LONDON   AUCKLAND   SYDNEY
MEXICO CITY   NEW DELHI   HONG KONG   BUENOS AIRES

IF YOU PURCHASED THIS BOOK WITHOUT A COVER, YOU SHOULD BE AWARE THAT THIS BOOK IS STOLEN PROPERTY. IT WAS REPORTED AS "UNSOLD AND DESTROYED" TO THE PUBLISHER, AND NEITHER THE AUTHOR NOR THE PUBLISHER HAS RECEIVED ANY PAYMENT FOR THIS "STRIPPED BOOK."

No PART OF THIS PUBLICATION MAY BE REPRODUCED, STORED IN A RE-TRIEVAL SYSTEM, OR TRANSMITTED IN ANY FORM OR BY ANY MEANS, ELEC-TRONIC, MECHANICAL, PHOTOCOPYING, RECORDING, OR OTHERWISE, WITHOUT WRITTEN PERMISSION OF THE PUBLISHER. FOR INFORMATION REGARDING PERMISSION, WRITE TO SCHOLASTIC INC., ATTENTION: PERMISSIONS DEPARTMENT, 555 BROADWAY, NEW YORK, NY 10012.

ISBN 0-439-24071-9

TEXT COPYRIGHT © 2001 BY H.B. GILMOUR AND RANDI REISFELD. ILLUSTRATIONS COPYRIGHT © 2001 BY SCHOLASTIC INC.

ALL RIGHTS RESERVED. PUBLISHED BY SCHOLASTIC INC.

SCHOLASTIC AND ASSOCIATED LOGOS ARE TRADEMARKS AND/OR REGISTERED TRADEMARKS OF SCHOLASTIC INC.

12 11 10 9 8 7 6 5 4 3 2 1   1 2 3 4 5 6/0

PRINTED IN THE U.S.A.
FIRST SCHOLASTIC PRINTING, SEPTEMBER 2001

CHAPTER ONE
THE RETURN

"Witch Island," people on the mainland called it.

Of course, none of them had ever dared set foot there. Few had even seen it clearly.

It was one of a dozen small islands off Lake Superior's frigid shore. The only one often surrounded by a mysterious gray mist.

This gloomy curtain made it impossible to see from a distance that the island abounded with lovingly tended gardens, enchanting stone cottages, and a quaint village brightly painted in a rainbow of joyful colors.

Coventry Island was its real name.

On a crisp day in early September an old man with paper-thin skin and nappy white hair and his apprentice, a beautiful young woman in a billowing blue cape, tramped through Coventry's forest, heading for the fog-shrouded lake.

The old man carried two suitcases. Both belonged to his companion, who, even in these dark pine woods, was wearing outlandishly large sunglasses. In preparation, no doubt, for this sudden trip to California she'd insisted upon.

He'd given up trying to walk beside her. He was content to lag behind, catching just a word or two of her jabbering.

"I don't see why you won't let me try it." The young woman spun around abruptly. "The Council said I must play a more active part in the girls' lives and training —"

"And indeed you will, Ileana." There was no pretending he hadn't heard her. She was an excellent clairvoyant, had been able to read minds since late adolescence. "In fact, wondrous witch, I have just the mission for you —"

"Goddess," Ileana corrected her aged teacher. "It's not fair. Not fair at all. You've said yourself that I'm far more talented than most guardians. And the twins, whose well-being I'm responsible for — while amazingly gifted young witches — are extremely difficult to control. Don't you see, Karsh, if I knew how to transmutate . . ."

Transmutation. There it was again. She was far too impulsive to be taught such an advanced skill. "Transmutation is the trackers' art, Ileana," he told her once again. "The art of changing one human being into another."

"Well, you're a tracker," she shot back at him. "Yet you turned that hulking madman into a smarmy snake."

"If you're speaking of Lord Thantos —" the ancient warlock began.

"Why not a turtle? A snail? A slug? Something easy to catch!" the young witch continued, gray-eyed and glorious in her zeal. "For goodness' sake, Karsh, you could have turned yourself — or that evil black-bearded beast, Thantos — into anyone!"

Shivering in his black velvet suit and slippers, the old man sighed. "It was the quickest, easiest spell I could think of," he explained again in his odd, raspy voice. "Lord Thantos had just —"

A fat orange cat curled round his legs, making it even harder for him to walk. "Shoo, Boris," he ordered.

"Come to me, my pet," the beautiful young witch called to the tabby. Boris leaped obediently into her arms. But not without snagging her flowing silk cape.

"Don't!" the weary old man warned. It was too late. Ileana's quick temper had already flared. She was midway through the spell. If he stopped her now, poor Boris would have become half cat, half wriggling worm — and who knew which half would be which?

So their march was further delayed as Karsh's headstrong pupil turned her cat into a caterpillar and then, at the old man's command, undid the spell.

"You see? I could as easily have turned Boris into a snake," she grumbled. "It was the first spell you taught me — when I was *ten years old*! A child's spell, Karsh, not one to stop Lord Thantos!

"Thantos is a murderer. He killed his own brother. We were supposed to bring him back to the island to stand before the Council." Ileana pulled her dark silk cape more tightly around her. "And we could have, if you'd changed him into something easy to catch. But noooo. You chose to turn your fellow tracker, the treacherous Lord Thantos, into a swift, slithering ribbon of vile reptile, who skittered through the underbrush to freedom. And that he is now, Karsh. Free, thanks to you. Free to work his evil magick on Apolla and Artemis. Free to capture and enslave them — mere children. Innocent. Defenseless."

Rubbish, Karsh thought. Apolla and Artemis — or Camryn and Alexandra, as they were now known — were neither innocent nor defenseless. They were fourteen years old, no longer children. And they had never been *mere* anythings.

Extraordinary young witches they were. Adolescent adepts swiftly awakening to their gifts. From the beginning much had been expected of them — twin daughters of Aron and Miranda, two of the most powerful and beloved practitioners of the craft.

Apolla — the strong, serene beauty now called Camryn — had been named for the mythical ruler of the sun, and Artemis — or Alexandra, the restless, rebellious one — for the ancient moon goddess.

Both were skilled, sometimes fierce, hunters. But like their namesakes, the girls shared a protective love of animals and children . . . of innocents in danger.

It was as if they still remembered, Karsh thought, the terrible time of their father's death, their mother's ruin, and their uncle's wild pursuit of them through the icy forests of Coventry Island. Their uncle, the powerful Lord Thantos.

Ah, but they were infants then, so tiny that Karsh had been able to hold them, one in each hand. Swiftly separated to save their lives, sent away from their birthplace, they'd been reared by protectors whom Karsh had chosen.

One child he had delivered to rural Crow Creek, Montana. The other to suburban Marble Bay, Massachusetts. Two thousand miles apart for fourteen years, neither had been aware of the other's existence. Yet three months ago, they'd found each other.

And within weeks of their meeting, it had become necessary for them to live together.

"Which is precisely what put them in harm's way . . . in Thantos's way!" Ileana, who had read Karsh's mind, blurted. "Their foul uncle was never interested in stealing just one of them. He's always wanted them both. They were of no use to him separately. Only together could they reach the great power and fierce magick that is their heritage. If you hadn't decided to unite them — without consulting me, of course — Thantos might never have found them. But thanks to you, the greedy assassin came close to capturing them —"

"He didn't succeed, Ileana. That's what matters."

"But he will! Oh, please, Karsh, please," she begged in a very un-Ileana-like way. "Teach me the secret of transmutation. I'd be so much more helpful to you and to them if I could turn myself into another person."

The exhausted tracker stared into the startling gray eyes of his charge. He studied her intently for a moment. "You disappoint me," he said after sifting through her thoughts. "It's not for Camryn and Alexandra that you ask this precious gift, it's to impress Brice Stanley!"

He took up their luggage and their journey again.

"That is so unfair!" Ileana, who'd discovered on her last trip to Los Angeles that Brice, her favorite movie star, was an accomplished warlock, now hurried to catch up with Karsh. "You only heard my very last idea," she accused. "A silly afterthought, that's all. It is for them. Thantos will surely try to lure them again —"

"I've heard enough," Karsh tried to silence her.

"If you had kept them apart, as I commanded, their bloodthirsty uncle would never have found them," she insisted. "Yet you won't give me what I need to save them."

"As you commanded?" The old tracker was rarely angry with the vain young witch. But he was cold and tired and his back ached from carrying her absurdly heavy luggage. "Of what use can the secrets of transmutation be to you?" he sneered at her. "Lord Thantos will *not* try again soon. Though he is their uncle and a warlock of immense wealth and power, he knows that we'll be near. Watching. Waiting. He knows he's wanted back here at the island and that, sooner or later, he must return to face the Unity Council. As for you, Ileana, you may suggest, propound, request, propose . . . but command me? Never!"

"But I am responsible for their safety. I am their guardian," she protested.

"As I am yours, though you seem to forget it often enough," the aged tracker grumbled.

With a sullen pout, Ileana turned her back on him. "If Thantos has gone into hiding, then he'll send someone else to snare the twins," she argued.

"Very good," Karsh said. "And who do you think he'll send?"

"That's easy. Someone Apolla and Arte —"

"Camryn and Alexandra!" he reminded her.

"All right. Someone *Camryn and Alexandra* will mistake for a friend," Ileana went on. "Thantos will send someone the guileless, giving girls are drawn to. Some desperate creature, a maimed animal or lost child, a troubled being who seems to need their protection or help. Someone who'll act caring and devoted, until the time comes for him —"

"Or her," Karsh suggested.

"Or her," Ileana agreed, "until the time comes for Thantos's messenger to deliver them up to the murderous fiend himself."

"Then someone must warn them," Karsh said.

"Of course," Ileana agreed too quickly. Then, "No!" she protested. "Not me! You can't be serious. I'm on my way to California. I'm meeting Brice Stanley."

"You were. And now you're not." Grinning, Karsh waved his bony fingers like a carnival magician. "Presto change-o! You're on your way to Marble Bay!"

CHAPTER TWO
THE BETRAYAL

This was the moment Alexandra Fielding had been dreading.

But no way was she going to let anyone know that. Especially not the two boneheads who had dragged her here.

Outside the pizza parlor, Alex stood defiantly between them — Camryn Barnes, the twin sister she barely knew, and Cam's tall, gangly best friend, Beth.

Cam's brother, Dylan, was also along. With two earrings in his right earlobe and his long blond hair tied back in a ponytail, Dylan had a streak of mischief in him that tickled Alex. Less than a year younger than them and a head taller, Dylan had come home from an X-treme sports camp just days ago — and seemed to have already adjusted to the weird state of affairs he'd walked into.

Weird? Definition: Finding out that your beloved older sister was not your biological sister but had been adopted. Way weird? Learning that they'd all — the 'rents plus Cam and her best bud, Beth — run into your adopted sibling's spitting image, Alexandra Fielding, two thousand miles from home. And, as if that weren't enough, discovering that your comfortable, cluttered, dirty-socks-smelling room had been disinfected and re-modeled while you were gone.

From Alex's point of view, Dylan's easy acceptance of all that totally made him the coolest member of the Barnes tribe. She liked the delight in his blue eyes now, as he watched his usually successful sister sweating to get her way.

"Oh, come on, Alex." Cam tossed back her gleaming reddish-brown hair, picked a speck off the cuff of her creamy cashmere sweater, and began to toy with the dainty, smiling-sun charm dangling from her necklace. "We'll grab a Coke and a slice and you'll finally get to meet the rest of my friends."

"You totally betrayed me. You lured me here under false pretenses." Alex's arms were stubbornly crossed. "You never mentioned meeting anyone —"

"Trust me, you're going to like them," her look-alike insisted.

"Right. If you like sugar substitutes." Dylan grinned. "You know, sickeningly sweet but capable of wiping out lab rats."

Cam shot her brother an evil look. "Ignore him, like everyone else does," she suggested.

"Anyway," her shadow, Beth, chimed in, "everyone's psyched about meeting you."

Alex caught sight of herself in the restaurant window. Choppy auburn hair splashed with blue streaks. Ratty cutoffs. Oversize sweatshirt. Skull necklace. And enough jangly bracelets on her wrist to make it look like she'd jammed her fist through a Slinky.

She was not as wild about her outfit as she had been this morning when she was trying to creep out Cam and Beth. No way, like major, all caps NW, was she marching into a place where their Galleria-garbed gang was panting to meet her.

Well, whose fault was it that she looked like a trailer-trash nightmare? Hadn't Cam's mom, Emily, offered her a new wardrobe for school — which started on Monday? But no, Alex had insisted on her own cruddy clothes, worn in the mix-'n'-match style she'd mastered since arriving in Massachusetts.

Arriving?

Arriving didn't begin to explain how she'd gotten here, Alex thought. She hadn't so much arrived as appeared. Shown up. Materialized.

One minute she had been sitting on the sunbaked steps of her tacky trailer in Crow Creek, Montana; the next she was knocking on the door of Camryn Barnes's classy casa in Marble Bay, Massachusetts. Camryn Barnes, a girl she'd randomly run into this summer, a stranger who just happened to have the same birthday as Alex and the same metallic-gray eyes and nowhere nose and sulky lips . . . and the same fear that something was wrong with her, that she was different, radically different, from other kids.

It turned out that they were twins.

Until the lab report came back, Alex hadn't wanted to believe it. Now there was no doubt.

She and Cam — a popular, peppy, preppy, soccer-playing rich kid — were identical. Two peas in a pod. Bookend babes. Mirror-image, matching sisters who'd never seen each other until Cam's vacationing family decided to do a fun afternoon at Big Sky, the bogus theme park in Montana where Alex just happened to work.

Then things moved awful fast. Awful *and* fast was more like it.

Alex's mom had died. This scrawny, old white-haired guy — Doc, Alex called him — showed up at the funeral. While Alex was panicked about what she'd do next, he gave her some sweet-smelling herb — skullcap, it was called — to calm her. It made her sleepy. The last thing she remembered was Doc saying he knew just the place for her.

And this was the place. Marble Bay, Massachusetts, home of Camryn Barnes — the stranger who'd turned out to be Alexandra Fielding's long-lost twin.

Tell that true tale to anyone and win a one-way ticket to the nuthouse.

Running a hand through her spiky, streaked hair, Alex turned away from the shop window. "Read my glossy purple lips," she said. "Pizza pig-out, yes. Meet my evil twin's friends, no."

That cracked Dylan up. "Hang tough, Als," he encouraged.

"Excuse me, little bro. What time's that haircut appointment?" Cam asked, squinting pointedly at the boy.

Dylan checked his watch. "Yikes. I'm late. Catch ya later, sistas." Flashing some hand signal he'd picked up at camp, he split.

Long, tall Beth, with her wiry hair and freckled face, rolled her eyes.

They've known each other so long that Beth acts like Dyl's her brother, Alex heard Cam thinking. She was getting used to picking up other people's thoughts, especially Cam's. They could do other things, too. Alex could make things move just by thinking about them. Cam could stun people into tripping, or tripping up, just by staring at them. And sometimes, if Cam worked it just right, her piercing eyes could actually set things on fire. They weren't just twins, she reminded herself. They were twin witches. How else could they explain all the weird stuff they could do and see and hear that other kids they knew so could not?

"T'Witches," Alex said aloud, and Cam chuckled.

Beth glanced at them accusingly. Something private had passed between them that she'd been left out of. Again.

"Laugh all you want," she said sourly to Alex. "Whatever Dylan says, this is where our friends from Marble Bay High do face time. I mean, what are you going to do when school starts, Alex — just only hang with Cam?"

Alex shrugged off the girl's chilly tone. It took work, she knew, for Beth Fish to frost anybody. Basically cheerful and easygoing, Beth was still hurting over Cam's instant bonding with Alex. Now she had to deal with Alex and Dylan's mutual admiration society.

Camryn Barnes, premonition princess, sensed it,

too. "This place is the pits, right, Beth?" Sharing an inside joke, Cam tried to reassure her best friend.

It worked. Beth giggled. "Pits. P-I-T-S," she spelled it out for Alex. "That's short for Pie In The Sky, remember?"

"How could I forget? Everything in this cutesy town has a cutesy name." Alex rolled her eyes — black-rimmed, silvery gray, identical to Cam's.

"Come on, Alex," Cam urged again. "I promised the Pack I'd introduce you —"

"The Pack, ugh." Alex wrinkled her nose at the lame name. "Talk about cutesy." The Six Pack was what Cam and her pals called themselves because there were, duh, six of them: Cam and Beth and four other girls —

"Only three are going to be here for sure," Cam said — just to show off, Alex figured, just to prove she could hear her twin's private thoughts.

Big whoop. Cam hadn't even known she could read minds until Alex showed up.

"Sukari, Amanda, and Kristen. Brianna may not make it," Cam continued. "She's expecting a call from her dad."

"Bree's dad lives on the West Coast." Beth twirled a finger around one of the thousand corkscrew curls that framed her freckled face. "He's this big Hollywood producer or something —"

Bree. Brianna. The name was familiar to Alex. Then she remembered. Bree was bulletin girl, the gushing gossip whose phone conversation Alex — with her extraordinary hearing, which had become even keener since meeting Cam — had overheard her first morning in Marble Bay. "Not Bree, the human Hoover. She who sucks up dirt —"

Beth giggled again. "You have to get to know her," she said, quickly switching gears. "I mean, Bree can sound all cutting and judgmental, but she's actually supersensitive, even if she acts harsh —"

"She probably won't even be here," Cam tried to reassure Alex, "but you'll really like Amanda, I think. And Sukari, who's like this total brainiac. And Kristen. Come on, Alex, you're going to meet them sooner or later. School starts day after tomorrow. Don't you want to know a few kids before you get there?"

"Excuse me?" Alex said. "What part of 'No Way' don't you understand? Want me to spell it out for you?"

A chill breeze swept by unexpectedly. The wave of frigid air raised goose bumps on Alex's arms and prickled the back of her neck.

"Cam?" she asked softly, rubbing her arms, feeling her jaw tighten against the cold. "Do you feel that?"

"Feel what?" Beth asked, looking around.

"Cold," Cam replied, "like a sudden drop in temperature. And — help!" Cam's shoulders hunched. She spun around fast. "Cut it out," she warned. "Who pulled my hair?"

Alex's eyes widened. "Did you say something?"

Annoyed, Beth folded her arms. "Duh. She said she's cold. And then, like, someone pulled her hair. Inside joke? I think so."

"Wait," Alex continued to Cam. "Didn't you also just say you had something important to tell me?"

"Oh, man. Not again. Not now," Cam groaned. But oops, there it was — she felt that icy chill. Alex obviously heard a voice, a voice that wasn't Cam's. Cam tried to keep it together. "I just wanted —"

"Ow!" It was Beth this time. She jumped about a foot off the ground, clutching her bottom. "Did you do that?" she demanded of Alex. "Because if you did, I think it's gross and totally rude."

"— I just wanted you to meet my friends," Cam finished her sentence on automatic.

Her twin's slightly shaky voice brought Alex back to the reality zone. Shivering, trying to figure out what was happening, she'd spaced. But she had definitely heard a sharp, oddly familiar voice say, *Ditch the frizzy-haired friend; I've got something important to say.*

So what was it going to be — dump Beth on command and wait out here in the arctic chill for something weird to happen or head inside where a bunch of spoiled but safe fourteen-year-olds were waiting to check her out?

No contest.

"Meet your pals? Fresh," Alex exclaimed. "Can't wait!" Taking Cam's and Beth's arms, she hurried into Pie In The Sky.

CHAPTER THREE
THE WARNING

The pizza shop was comfortingly busy. From just inside the door, Alex inspected the noisy place, while Cam checked the big booth near the front window that was practically the property of the Six Pack.

"They're not here yet," she said. "Are we early?"

"Just lucky," Alex cracked.

Beth checked her watch. "Five minutes late," she reported, "thanks to Sister Dearest."

A waitress in sandals and sunglasses sauntered over to the girls. She looked at Beth. "Ugh. You've got something stuck in your teeth," the waitress told the rangy girl. "Something green and gross."

"Oh, no!" Beth frantically brushed a finger back and

forth over her front teeth. "How heinous. Did I have it all the time we were outside?"

"I don't see —" Cam began, as Beth bolted for the bathroom.

"Over there, kids," the waitress cut in, pointing to the tiny table wedged into the back corner, directly under the noisy dripping air-conditioning unit.

"Are you new?" Cam asked.

"What's that supposed to be, a blond joke?" the waitress demanded.

"No way," Cam said, reddening. "It's just that I'm, you know, like a regular here and I've never seen you before and, like, I always sit at the big booth."

"She's expecting friends," Alex explained.

"Believe me, girls, your party has arrived."

"Uh, do I know you?" Cam stared at the waitress. "There's something so familiar about you."

Ever since her twin's arrival, all of Cam's senses had become sharper, but most especially her sight. Now she squinted hard at the waitress's sunglasses.

At first she saw only her own reflection in the dark lenses. Then the supersight she'd developed lately kicked in. The lenses began to lighten until they were almost as transparent as ordinary glasses. And she saw the waitress's eyes. They were gray, a fierce and fiery gray, outlined in black.

Cam gasped. "O.M.G.! Your eyes. You have the same eyes as us! Are you . . . ?"

"No, no, no, no!" The waitress stepped back, offended. "Spare me. Don't even go there! For goodness' sake, do I look *old enough* to be your mother?!"

"How did you know what she was thinking?" Alex demanded.

"But your eyes," Cam said. "I only know one other person with those eyes. Not counting Alex, of course."

"Officer Ileana!" Finally, Alex had been able to place the voice.

"Call me Goddess," their waitress instructed.

They'd met her once before, Alex realized. She'd been dressed as a policewoman that time. She was the bony man's partner — the old man who Alex knew as Doc and Cam called the bleacher-creature. He'd been in a police uniform, too, the first time they saw him together. His badge had identified him as Officer Karsh.

Whatever his real name was, he had come to them in dreams all through their strange, separated childhood. And only a month ago, he and his beautiful young colleague had saved them from the hulking, bearded bad guy in the hobnail boots. Officer Ileana, this very waitress, this stunning woman, had called the sadistic liar — who'd said he could take them to their birth mother — a dangerous maniac and a murderer.

"Over there," Ileana said now, shooing the twins toward the isolated table under the air conditioner. "We'll need privacy."

"Are you undercover?" Cam asked.

"More like underappreciated," Ileana replied sullenly. "Let's go. Move it."

"No." Cam bristled unexpectedly. "It's too noisy, too cold, and our friends are meeting us up front."

"They'll be late," the waitress said and, when Cam looked at her curiously, she added, "The roads around here are awful. They probably got a flat or something."

Grasping Alex's arm, Cam turned on her heels and headed for the Six Pack's booth next to the front window.

"I told Karsh you were difficult," Ileana said, following them.

"I am not difficult," Cam grumbled over her shoulder.

"Sit!" Ileana commanded.

Obediently, Cam and Alex slid into the booth. They sat facing the plate-glass storefront. Daylight streaming in the wide window hurt Cam's sensitive gray eyes. Alex squinted up at Ileana, who stood looming over the table, menus in hand.

"I'd like a diet Coke and —" Cam began.

"I am not here to take your orders," the sunglasses-wearing waitress cut her off. "*Au contraire*. I'm here to issue some. A warning, actually. You remember —"

"Ileana . . . Goddess . . . whatever. You were the one who whispered to me outside, right?" Alex asked.

"And pulled my hair?" Cam added, narrowing her eyes at the frustrated witch.

"Wake up and smell the pepperoni. I was trying to get your attention," Ileana hissed back through gritted teeth. "A task I'm still working on."

"Well, you didn't have to pull my hair," Cam insisted.

But Alex's attention was sidetracked by someone walking past Pie In The Sky — a long-limbed boy wearing faded jeans and a black jacket so old and worn that the leather was flaking.

He was a total babe, definitely, but beyond that . . . there was something about him that made Alex's heart quicken, that heated her chilled blood and set her face aflame.

The boy seemed to sense that someone was watching him. He glanced at the window, straining to see inside. His intense eyes, ringed by pitch-black lashes, were cool and blue.

Whipping off her glasses, Ileana fixed Cam with a gray-eyed glare. "All I ask is five uninterrupted minutes of your precious time. Five minutes of your undivided attention. If you'd caught my drift outside this Parmesan palace, it would've been a lot easier — on me. But noooo. Why should anyone make things easy for me!

Okay, here's the drill. I came to warn you. Someone will come to you offering friendship, praise, love . . . whatever you find attractive —"

"Wow, who was that?" Alex watched leather boy move out of sight.

"Hello!" Ileana roared. "I'm speaking to you — both of you! I didn't pop in for the garlic knots! I'm here to warn you against —"

"Warn us against what?" Alex asked, tuning back in to the conversation.

"Listen to me!" the witch-waitress ordered. "I haven't much time left. You met him once, the renegade tracker in the hobnail boots. He's a murderer. And a coward. Since he dares not show his bearded face again, he'll send someone else to lure you to him. Beware, then — of anyone trying to get close to you, anyone who seems drawn to you. And" — she looked pointedly at Alex — "anyone you feel drawn to."

Bearded face. Hobnail boots. The guy who tried to get them this summer, Cam remembered.

Beth was heading for their booth. "There was totally nothing in my teeth," she grumbled.

Cam and Alex exchanged guilty glances, then turned back to Ileana.

The kitchen's swinging door flapped loudly. The haughty waitress was gone.

Sitting between Cam and the wall, Alex tried to slide out of the booth to follow her. "Move," she implored her twin.

"Oh, no," Cam said. She was looking out the window at a trio of laughing girls piling out of a red SUV. "Great timing. My crew is here."

Alex glanced once more at the kitchen door, but she knew Ileana had left the building.

"What did you tell your friends?" Alex wanted to know.

Cam shrugged. "Nothing much."

"Just about Montana, Alex. And that you two are sisters and how her mom isn't your mom but maybe your mom is hers. Nothing much." Beth laughed.

"I didn't say we were twins," Cam added mischievously.

"Oh, I forgot," Alex said, "you like building a mystery."

"Oh, and you don't?"

"Hey, Cam." A tall, good-looking boy in a waiter's apron was striding toward their table. "I didn't see you come in. Hey, hi, Beth. How's it going, uh, Alex, right?"

She'd met him before. Jason was his name. He was going into his final year at Marble Bay High, Alex remembered. A hottie with a driver's license, who'd helped them out of a jam a couple of weeks ago. Jason, the lovesick senior who was all crushed out on Cam.

"Oh, hi, Jase." Cam threw him a smile. It wasn't a hundred-watt halogen, but the boy seemed satisfied.

"What can I get you guys?" he asked, not taking his eyes off Cam.

"Um, where's . . . the new waitress?" Beth asked, peering around him. "Blond with sunglasses, likes to play tricks on unsuspecting customers?"

Jason was clueless. "There is no new waitress," he said.

CHAPTER FOUR
BUILDING A MYSTERY

Cam's friends stormed the table. They were all talking at once, complaining about the flat they'd gotten on the way over, teasing Jason, high-fiving Beth, ragging on Cam about the soccer game she'd blown the day before summer vacation, and demanding to know what her big surprise was.

Then they saw Alex.

"Who . . . I mean, what . . . ?" The gracefully athletic Asian-American girl with the glossy black braid actually clutched her heart and took a step backward. "Is this a joke?"

Who's the neat freak? Alex wondered, taking in the

girl's fresh white tee, crisp khakis, and spotless white sneakers.

Telepathically, Cam did the cheat sheet. *Kristen Hsu,* she silently told Alex. *She's artistic . . . very into computer graphics. Which, I guess, is kind of precise and orderly —*

What a relief, Alex responded. *Knowing that we'll have so much in common.*

Eyes and mouth wide open, Kristen turned to see whether the others had checked out Alex yet.

"So, uh, you guys are . . . related." Sukari Woodward, pretty, plump, and brown-skinned, sporting granny glasses and a peroxide-blond 'fro, laughed out loud at herself. "Brilliant, right? Just me keepin' it real."

"And that, folks," Cam narrated, "was the hypothesis of Dr. Sukari Woodward, brainiac and science buff."

"Related?!" Kristen cracked up. "It's like the Olsens on steroids!"

"You met her in a theme park in Montana?" Sukari said. "Dag, what was it called, Xerox-land? Do they make copies of everyone who goes there?"

"No," Kristen said, "I bet they have a ride called the Cy-*clone.* Get it, clone?"

"Well, I think it's cosmic," a whispery voice noted. "Totally astral." This from the third member of the trio — a sunny redhead in earthy sandals, a gauzy Indian-print sarong, and one long feather earring peeking through her tangle of curls. "You two look almost identical."

"It's the blue streaks," Beth pointed out. "Whoops. Cam doesn't have any."

"No, really, Cami," the redhead said, "she is so the yin to your yang!"

"Ladies and gentlemen, Amanda Carter," Cam reported.

Laughing, 'Manda took a seat.

Jason took their orders.

Sukari took over the bench on Beth's side of the booth.

And Kristen took out her cell phone and speed-dialed Bree.

They had been warned. The bearded psycho in the heavy boots was trying to find them. He couldn't go after them himself, so he was sending someone else. "And we're supposed to watch out for what?" Cam asked on the way to school two days later.

"Anyone who's drawn to us or who we're drawn to," Alex recited.

"Kind of cramps your social life," Cam observed as a crossing guard signaled that they could step off the curb now.

"After meeting your crew, that's fine with me," Alex cracked.

A block away, the plaza in front of Marble Bay High was swarming with kids. All of them strangers to her, except for Dylan, who had left for school with his own pals. And five of Cam's Dirty Half Dozen, which was one of the names Alex had started calling the Six Pack. The Lollipop League was another. And the Jellybean Jar.

"Dag, it must feel whack," she remembered Sukari saying, "leaving all your homeys behind."

And then Kristen, twirling her silky black braid like a bullwhip, going, "Duh, didn't you hear her, Suki? She only had two friends in Wyoming. Lulu and Evan —"

"Montana," Amanda had corrected in her breathless little whisper. "And it was Lucinda, not Lulu. Lucinda and Evan. Anyway, that's not what she meant, Kristen. You meant you only had two *best* friends, right, Ali?"

Red curls, ebony braid, peroxide-blond 'fro. They looked more like they belonged in a jellybean jar than a soda pop Six Pack, Alex remembered thinking.

She'd had a monster headache by the time they left PITS. And so had Cam, they discovered, when they compared notes on the way home.

By the time they'd reached Cam's house, the worst of Alex's pain had let up. Only to be replaced by a bigger headache: Dylan.

Cam's cutie-pie brother had decided to have his long blond locks chopped — and streaked blue — like Alex's. Which had totally put Cam's mother Emily into orbit.

Though even Cam had admitted last night that Dyl looked buff in his new 'do, Emily had glared daggers at Alex all through dinner.

"Come on, let's review," Cam said now, as they turned onto the school's wide central walkway. She pointed discreetly. "They're all over there."

Alex groaned, but complied. "Okay, so the curvy, cocoa-skinned blond in the granny glasses is Sukari. Black-haired, slightly edgy Chinese-American, that's Kristen. Kristen Hsu, right? And the pale redhead in hippie-dippy retro wear is Amanda. Beth is Beth. And . . . whoa! That's gotta be Bree. She looks exactly like her voice — all tight and screechy!"

There was something about the short, skinny girl — from the blond streaks in her expertly highlighted hair to the oh-so-cool perfection of her platform slides — that hit Alex like nails on a blackboard. Lucinda and Evan had an expression for the type. "T-cubed." Too. Totally. Trendy.

Brianna was waiting for them, Kristen at her side, at the arched front entrance to the school. "Wait. Don't tell me," the petite girl drawled, extending a tennis-bracelet-bedecked arm. "You must be Alexandra." She peered over her sunglasses and looked Alex up and down like a pint-sized inspector grading meat. "Why, you look exactly like —"

"Cam?" Beth prompted facetiously.

"Excuse me?" Brianna raised an eyebrow at Cam's tall, frizzy-haired best. "Did I call for a ventriloquist? I move my mouth, and *you* do the talking? I don't think so."

"Dag," Sukari laughed. "She dissed your butt, Beth."

"I was going to say," Bree finished, pointedly ignoring Sukari, "that you look *exactly* like Kris described you."

"Oh, really? And how's that?" Cam asked, flashing a warning glare at Brianna.

"Indescribably weird!" Bree answered, offering her palm to Kristen for a high five.

Cam glanced quickly at Alex. No words, spoken or unspoken, were necessary for her to read her twin's intentions. Alex's gray eyes had flicked to the freshly hosed bottom of the archway, specifically to the shallow puddle of water coating the marble slab on which Bree stood. *No*, Cam thought. *Oh, Alex, don't!*

I'm cool, her grinning twin silently assured her. And actually, Alex's eyes were cool, furiously frosty, as she watched Bree skid suddenly on a glass-smooth slick of ice that had somehow formed beneath her feet.

Bree teetered and twirled, reaching out for balance.

Kristen ducked, trying to get out of her way, but Bree's flailing hand caught her and sent her crashing back against one of the great oak doors thrown open to welcome Marble Bay High students. Kristen slid to the ground, the door at her back, her long legs splayed before her.

Stop it! Cam silently scolded Alex.

Oh, all right, her twin groused. A nanosecond later, Bree flopped down, hitting the ice-coated marble with a resounding *thwack.*

Cam and Beth helped her to her feet, while Amanda and Sukari, both giggling, hoisted Kris.

"Nothing bruised but my pride," Brianna assured everyone, dusting off her skirt. She glanced at Alex, studied her suspiciously for a second, then shrugged and announced, "However, a lawsuit is not out of the question."

Ten minutes later, they were all inside, hangin' in the hallway at the tenth-grade lockers. While Cam and company caught up with school friends, Alex fiddled with the lock Emily had given her. She was trying to remember the combination; she had the first two turns down, but wasn't sure of the third.

A pleasant scent of soap and leather muddled her thinking. Before she could trace it, a hoarse voice offered, "I can open it for you, if you've lost the combo."

Alex looked up into the cool blue eyes of the leather-jacketed boy she'd seen walking past the pizza shop.

"That's okay. I know the combination." Suddenly Dylan was at her side. "You're new around here, right? I'm Dylan Barnes."

"Yeah, we moved here in July. Cade Richman," the boy introduced himself. He looked from Dylan back to Alex, taking in their blue streaks and look-alike haircuts. "Oh, are you two . . . ?"

"Oh, no. Definitely not. He's my brother," Alex explained. "Actually, he's not even *my* brother, he's my *sister's* brother. I'm Alex Fielding." Cade was staring at her, bewildered but amused. Alex laughed. "It's a long story."

He scratched his head, his hair a tumble of ink-dark curls. "Sounds complicated," he said with a crooked smile. "Okay, well, nice meeting you guys."

"I'm new, too," Alex called after him.

"Cool." He waved. "Catch you at orientation."

She looked up. Six faces, mouths open, eyes wide, were staring at her.

"Who was that?" Beth was the first to cross the hall.

"His name's Cade —" Dylan started to answer.

Kristen brushed away his attempt. "Cade Richman. Rumors are already flying about the boy. Got kicked out of some other school and dumped here. He's trouble."

"I never saw him before and hope never to again," Brianna insisted. "Coffee, chocolate, boys — some things are just better rich. I mean, torn jeans, that cruddy leather jacket, and those mountain-man boots? Please, so not my type."

"Mmm," Sukari countered. "Tall, tasty, and intense — he's totally mine."

"Only it's Alex who cast a spell over him," Amanda teased.

Alex locked eyes with the feather-earringed redhead.

"Don't mind 'Manda," Sukari told her. "She's, like, all into chanting, scented candles, and simmering herbs. She's our local witch."

"Right. When Camryn isn't doing her mojo thing," Beth added, grinning at her best. Cam's mojo was what the Six Pack called the uncanny vibes, hunches, and premonitions their bud was known for. Until last season's championship match. When the soccer ace had suddenly suffered a space-out in the final moments of the Marble Bay Meteors' most important game.

"Oh, you mean like during . . . soccer play-offs?" Bree purred innocently.

Amanda gasped.

"Put a sock in it, Bree," Sukari ordered.

"Or what?" Bree laughed. "Gonna get 'Manda to put a hex on me?"

Beth and Kristen apprehensively watched Cam, who seemed unaware of the rumpus around her. "Did you see his boots, Als?" she murmured. "He was wearing boots."

Alex looked down the hall again. Cade was leaning against another bank of lockers, looking, as Sukari had put it, tasty and intense. And, no, she hadn't noticed before, but he was wearing boots, scuffed black motorcycle boots.

Alex forced herself to laugh. "Sure, like a gazillion other guys in the world," she told Cam. "That doesn't make him . . . you know, bad to the bone."

But she'd picked up on Cam's train of thought: The killer, the big, bearded bozo they'd been warned about, wore boots, heavy, clunky boots, even in the sweltering summer.

So did that mean whoever he sent to snag them would share his fondness for funky footwear? No way, Alex decided, determined to get inside Cade's head, to prove Cam wrong.

But she couldn't. The buff boy's mind was murky and shut down. There was something stirring there in the dark, a devastating secret, which Alex couldn't decode. She couldn't read it, she realized, because Cade refused to think about it. He was hiding something, not just from her, but from himself.

Cam was on a similar mission. Cade was a stranger. Only Kristen seemed to know something about him — and that wasn't much. Except he was clearly someone Alex was attracted to, and his boots had reminded Cam of the scary guy they'd met the night Ileana and Officer Karsh had rescued them.

Was Cade the murderer's messenger?

Cam's sight grew hazy. The hall chaos faded as a pounding in her ears got louder. She trembled, though she knew what was happening. It had happened before she'd met Alex, but never with the intensity she'd experienced since.

She was about to see or know something that she couldn't possibly see or know.

Cam's stomach knotted. Then . . .

There was a blur of red metal. Headlights speeding toward her. A car hurtling along a narrow road. High-pitched voices, screaming . . . laughing.

A hand grabbed hers. Cam gasped, but forced her eyes open. "Did you see it?" she whispered to Alex, who was holding on to her.

"No," her sister answered softly, truthfully. "I tried, but I couldn't see anything."

CHAPTER FIVE
A CLASH IN THE CORRIDOR

"You guys," Brianna called impatiently, "we're going to the lunchroom. Are you coming?"

"In a minute," Alex said. The hallway was becoming more crowded. "You look terrible," she whispered to Cam.

"It's not my fault we're identical," Cam answered with a weak grin. "We'll meet you downstairs," she told her waiting friends.

"Whatever." Beth sounded annoyed.

A couple of Dylan's friends passed. "Later," he said, taking off after them as the rest of the Six Pack joined the flow of students heading for the cafeteria.

"I saw something," Cam confided as soon as they were out of sight. "But I have no idea what it meant or whether it had anything to do with the warning we got." Wiped out, she leaned back against the wall.

"It's okay. Just breathe," Alex advised. "We can figure it out later."

Kids streamed by, sharing summer stories, comparing homeroom assignments and class schedules. Here and there small groups gathered, causing jams that slowed the flow.

A series of cries — "Hey, watch it!" "Look out!" "Yo, chill, bro!" — followed one boy's path. He was large, with small, mean eyes and a bristly shaved head. Behind him a zoo of jocks followed, egging him on.

"Who is that?" Alex asked as the broad-chested guy elbowed through the crowd. "The dude's neck is bigger than my waist."

"Eddie Robins," Cam answered. "He's on the football team. He's kind of a jerk."

"Whoa," Alex teased. "He must really be evil for you to say that. I mean, you're so the un-Bree."

Then, a grinning Eddie viciously shouldered a mousy girl in thick glasses who was half his size.

"Evil enough?" Cam asked. The blow sent the elfin creature reeling. Kids jumped out of the way, gasped, shrank back, trying not to trample her, while Eddie's drooling gorillas hooted and elbowed one another. The heavy books the girl had been cradling flew out of her hands and skittered along the floor; her cheery red purse fell, too, bursting open on impact and sending its contents clattering every which way.

In the pandemonium, Eddie swooped down. "Let me give you a hand," he snickered, snatching the girl's bright plastic billfold. "Let's see, any ID in here?"

Is he actually going to take her money? Alex wondered, outraged.

Right here in broad daylight, Cam thought, starting to boil. *In the middle of the hall with . . .*

Everyone just standing around watching! Alex couldn't believe it.

The girl was on her knees, gathering up her books. On her skinny wrist she wore a man-sized watch; its band was inches too big for her. She was shaking.

As if in sympathy, Alex began to tremble, too. An icy wave of anger, she guessed, swept through her, setting her teeth chattering.

Some kids had knelt to help retrieve the frail girl's books and purse. A few reached out to the waif, but Eddie's pals jeered at them, and the victim's head was down. She either didn't see the decent kids or, too embarrassed, simply ignored their hands. But no one would go near Eddie, who was rifling through her wallet. He pulled out a bus pass. "'Madison Knudnik,'" he read.

"What's the matter, Edgar, your old man dock your allowance again?" someone in the crowd called out in a soft, sandpapery voice that Alex recognized.

"It's Cade," she breathed.

The bully looked up, his eyes narrowed at the new boy, but he signaled his troops to cool out. "Yo, Richie Rich Boy. You think my old man's like yours? Mine don't make the big bucks —"

"They know each other," Cam realized.

"Are you angry enough to scorch that skank Eddie?" Alex asked her. "Give him a hot flash? Or do you need a little help?"

"Right here, you want me to do it? In front of half the school?"

"Well, I wasn't thinking of introducing you as the Fabulous Flame-o or anything. I thought maybe you could be subtle about it," Alex hissed.

Cade was moving through the crowd, trying to get near Eddie.

"Go, girl," Alex urged Cam. "Or are you waiting for me to ice the hallway?"

"Could you?" Cam pleaded.

"Do your best. Or your worst." Alex squeezed her twin's hand. "Barbecue the beefy loser."

Camryn closed her eyes for a moment, then opened them, focusing full-out on Eddie Robins. Her eyes began to sting; her face grew flushed; her hand gripped Alex's so hard that Alex let out a yelp of pain.

The girl on the floor heard it and glanced up. She blew a strand of limp brown hair from her forehead. She had a long nose and thin lips, which curled suddenly in a strange smile. Her sad, dark eyes widened at the sight of the twins as if she recognized them.

The sound of Eddie's breathing, shallow and fast now, almost as if he were panting, made Alex turn away from Madison. Eddie had started to blink rapidly. His face and fleshy neck began to sweat. Loosening his T-shirt collar and mopping his forehead, he searched the crowd, looked up toward the heat vents, wondering what was going on.

Just as Cade broke through the circle of kids surrounding the bully, Cam focused and a searing blast of fiery air brought Eddie to his knees. He covered his eyes and screamed, "What'd you do to me, Richman? I'm blind. I can't see. My eyes are burning. I'll get you for this!"

"Man, j'ya see that?" some of the startled jocks were grumbling. "Yo, what'd ya do to him?" A few moved menacingly in Cade's direction, but Eddie hollered, "Gimme a hand here!" and they backed off quickly.

After pulling Madison to her feet, Cade picked up

the wallet Eddie had dropped and returned it to the petite girl.

People started pressing forward, slapping his back, trying to shake his hand, shouting, "Whew, that was ultimate cool, man," and "How'd you do that?"

Cade looked around, over the heads of the kids encircling him. Catching Alex's eye, he shrugged and smiled at her, as if to say, *I don't know what's going on here, honest*, then turned away.

Madison ran right past him, moving straight for Cam and Alex. Her squeaky voice added to her mousy aspect. "You're the ones who rescued Marleigh Cooper!"

It was true, but hardly anyone knew it.

Weeks ago, America's pop princess had been kidnapped. Cam and Alex had used their budding powers to find the teen singing sensation and win her release.

Thanks to Camryn's dad, David Barnes — your basic one-in-a-million, good-guy lawyer — their names had not been leaked to the press. Dave wouldn't allow them to be photographed or give interviews. So, as far as most people were concerned, a pair of gutsy teenage girls who preferred to remain anonymous had saved Cooper.

How did this newcomer know about their role in Marleigh's rescue?

"Oh, wow," the hyper girl continued. "How neat.

I'm Madison. I'm new here. And sooo lost. But big-time. Gosh, you're both sooo pretty. Imagine that. Like, brave *and* beautiful. It's not fair. Just kidding. I've got orientation first period and I don't even know where the auditorium is —"

What's that face for? Alex silently asked Cam, who was looking at Madison as if the girl really were a small rodent or bothersome bug.

Cam rubbed her forehead. *It's just, I'm . . . Don't mind me, Als, I have a killer headache. I'm not thinking straight.*

A couple of Eddie's pals had him on his feet again. Angrily, he shook off their hands. Just before he lumbered down the hall, he glanced over his shoulder.

I'll get you! Alex heard him thinking. It wasn't hard to read his mind; he was staring directly at them.

"I don't guess you guys could, like, take me there?" Madison was saying. She nibbled her words fast and furiously, like a mouse eating cheese. "I'm just kinda nervous. You know, 'cause of what just went down."

"No big," Alex said. "I'm going there, too. It's just down those stairs, I think." She turned to Cam for confirmation.

Cam nodded. "First floor, south."

"Catch ya later," Alex said.

Madison grinned hugely. "You guys are so stellar. I can't believe it. My first day of school and I get to meet the two coolest girls in Marble Bay. Wow."

Cam watched them making their way down the hall. Something about the fragile girl disturbed her, something other than her smallness, manic chatter, and cheerful neediness. But Cam's eyes still stung and her head ached and she couldn't put her finger on what it was exactly that troubled her about Madison Knudnik.

CHAPTER SIX
A GRIEVOUS ERROR

A note from Lady Rhianna, head of the Unity Council, Coventry Island's high court, awaited Ileana on her return.

"Oh, beans," the impatient witch grumbled, unfurling the rolled and ribboned parchment that had been tacked to her cottage door. "Now what?" She read the document, then let it curl back up like a snapped window shade. "It's bad enough you've been barking at me since I landed, now Lady Potato wants a go at me, too."

"Ileana!" Karsh scolded, setting her bags down next to Boris, who was napping on the slate doorstep.

"Oh, all right. Lady Rhianna, then. But for goodness' sake, Karsh, she's round, lumpy, and brown — and clearly she has eyes everywhere. Or should I say *spies* everywhere?" Ileana plopped herself onto the big cosmetics case, crossed her delicate arms, and breathed an exaggerated sigh.

"Anyway, *I* didn't choose the pizza place," she declared after a pause. "They did, Apolla and Artemis —"

"Camryn and Alexandra," he reminded her.

"Whatever! They chose the place, your headstrong little fledglings. I tried to get their attention outside —"

"By pulling Camryn's hair and pinching her friend's bottom?" Biting his lip to keep from smiling, Karsh shook his head gravely.

"By any means necessary," Ileana shot back. "Why should I be cautious when Thantos will not be? And what's so wrong with having our little chat in a pizza parlor anyway? They needed to be warned about Thantos's messenger."

"Ileana, you interfered with the lives of three innocents. Four, counting the mother who was driving —"

"Innocents?" she argued. "It was just a flat tire. And did you see how they behaved when I was gone? Shrieking, stuffing their mouths, spitting straw wrappers at their peers —"

"We don't do that!" Karsh cut her short. "It is forbidden. We don't enchant, cast spells upon, or otherwise meddle in the lives of others — except for their good, not ours."

"Well, two of my charges were in grave danger. Two who are worth more than all the others combined —"

"Never," Karsh exclaimed, shocked. "Such a notion is unworthy of a true witch. It is totally against our beliefs. All life is sacred —"

A flapping of wings overhead startled Ileana. She tumbled off her perch, landing on Boris's tail. The sleeping cat screeched. Scrambling wildly, he dashed into the woods.

"Ah, there you are. Punctual as ever!" Lady Rhianna dipped low over the cottage. "To the Justice Dome — now! — if you please," she ordered.

"I'm as punctual as you are patient," Ileana grumbled, getting to her feet and swatting leaves and twigs from her silk cape. "I just arrived and found your summons."

Karsh hooded his eyes with one raw-knuckled white hand. With the other, he waved warmly to Rhianna. Soaring above them, she looked like a beautiful blimp, he thought, admiring her dimpled, bronze face and sparkling black eyes, her wiry gray hair, which smelled of almond oil. Most of all, he admired her glorious wings. Only a few years younger than he, and she could still manage those stunning appendages — each of which weighed nearly as much as Karsh did.

Lady Rhianna smiled at him. "I'll see you — both," she emphasized, "in my chambers. Karsh, old friend, you look weary."

"I wish he was," Ileana sulked.

Rhianna's head snapped toward the young witch. Her eyes darkened; her wings flapped once, threateningly.

"I merely meant I wish he were weary of *lecturing me*," Ileana quickly explained. "Of course, he could have taught me to transmutate. I'd almost talked him into it —"

"Transmutation?" Rhianna roared.

Karsh flinched. "But I didn't," he pointed out.

Rhianna studied him for a moment, then wheeling abruptly, flew off.

"You're in trouble, aren't you?" Ileana laughed.

"Not as much as if I'd given you your way." His knees creaking uncomfortably, the old warlock lowered himself onto the warm doorstep. "You're a guardian, Ileana — quicker and more talented than most, a truly gifted practitioner of magick. Still, you had no right to alter —"

"Alter, shmalter! I flattened a tire on that red gas guzzler. No one got hurt. That big show-off can wait. I'm going to rinse the stench of tomatoes and garlic off me.

Then I'll give you a lift to the Justice Dome. Rest awhile," Ileana suggested. Moving past him into her cottage, she let her hand play delicately over his cottony hair.

Karsh smiled, surprised. The reckless young witch he'd pledged to safeguard had touched him — not just with her hand, but with her heart as well.

Her gentle gesture and kind instinct gladdened him. For too long Karsh had feared Ileana was her father's child. He closed his wind-stung eyes now — just for a moment.

He was jarred awake when Ileana cried out, "Last stop!" and, opening her arms, let him fall to the frost-crisp ground in front of the Justice Dome.

Karsh landed upright on his spindly legs. Ileana had seen to that. She'd also made sure that Lady Rhianna and her deputy, Lord Grivveniss, had witnessed their arrival — and noted how very talented she was.

Not many guardians her age could levitate, let alone fly. But Karsh had encouraged Ileana to try her wings earlier than most. Naturally, Ileana's wings were not as showy or grand as Lady Rhianna's. Still, they were adorable and tastefully dusted with gold.

The esteemed elders were waiting before the purple, red, and gold dome. Grivveniss, with his wispy goatee and bottle-thick glasses, hobbled toward her, applauding. "A remarkable landing for one so young, especially in such gusty weather," he congratulated Ileana.

She smiled at the old man. "I'm glad it pleases you," she said with enough sweet cream in her voice to set his cholesterol soaring. "It is my desire to become a tracker, my lord, as wise and skilled as you."

Lady Rhianna exchanged a skeptical look with Karsh, then loudly cleared her throat. "Yes, well, shall we get on with it?"

"By all means," Grivveniss agreed, offering Ileana his arm.

It was all she could do not to stick out her tongue as she glided past Karsh and his frumpy friend.

"I summoned you to find out why the innocents in Massachusetts were endangered," Rhianna began, once they were all seated in her chambers. "I understand they were friends of Apolla and Artemis."

Ileana grinned gleefully at Karsh.

"They're called Camryn and Alexandra now," he gently informed the head of the Unity Council.

"Thank you," she said shortly. "But now I want to hear about this flat-tire business. Whose bright idea was that?"

"Mine," Ileana confessed with no shame. "You and the Council wanted me to take more responsibility for the twins, wanted a more hands-on approach —"

"Esteemed elder," Karsh cut in. "The method was Ileana's, but the instructions were mine. I am but an aged servant —"

"Karsh, my dear, there are no servants among us. We are all lords and ladies, people with special gifts meant for the greater good of humankind."

"Of course. And it is in that spirit, Rhianna, that I allowed Ileana to go alone to Marble Bay and, by any means necessary, warn the fledglings of imminent danger. I am very old and she is young and strong —"

"Strong-willed."

"Did you not see how she carried Lord Karsh in her arms?" Grivveniss asked, smiling adoringly at Ileana.

"Indeed I did. As I was meant to. But why," Rhianna demanded, easing her silk-swaddled bulk from the chair, "did you have to create a hazardous accident?"

"The visit was to warn the girls that Lord Thantos would likely send someone to lure them. Someone who looked and acted like an ordinary being. And I approached them on their way to the restaurant, Large Lady, but even then they were with a friend. They're very popular, you know —"

"Large Lady?" Rhianna's wings ruffled menacingly but did not fly open.

"Did I say 'large'? I meant 'great.'"

Rhianna glanced at Karsh, then began to pace, her

gold cape flaring, her little red shoes clacking loudly on the marble floor. "You aren't seriously considering teaching the child transmutation, old friend?"

Karsh did not answer immediately. He could not say what he felt in his bones. That age was claiming him, dulling his senses and robbing him of strength far faster than he had expected. He felt a desire to pass along what he knew. No, not a desire, an urgent need. If Ileana was to take up her true guardianship of the twins, she'd have to learn more of the trackers' art. Much more — and more quickly.

"I see." Rhianna had, of course, heard his musings. Her gaze softened. Her eyes glistened, as if with tears, as they took in Karsh's feeble but familiar form. Then, remembering her rank, she cleared her throat and continued. "I can't believe you considered for even a moment teaching this rash and reckless young witch a tracker's secret. Now that I know, what am I to do?"

"What you must," Karsh offered. "Whatever you think best."

"Good Karsh." Lady Rhianna's booming voice broke, lowered to a whisper. "I cannot . . . I will not punish you for wanting to speed this vain and impatient guardian's education. But causing a blowout? A burst tire? No, no, no. We are dealing with human beings here — which requires maturity, honor, good sense —"

"All of Lord Thantos's fine qualities," Ileana said insolently.

"Child," Grivveniss said kindly, "while many share your belief that Lord Thantos was responsible for the death of Aron, the twins' father —"

"Who was," Lady Rhianna reminded her, "Thantos's own brother."

"His brother . . . as if that made his evil act less possible! Also his business partner," Ileana added emphatically, "creator of a computer empire worth billions of dollars in the world beyond this speck of an island. Might not such riches be motive enough for murder?"

"Indeed," Grivveniss agreed. "But Lord Thantos had an alibi. An alibi sworn to by Miranda — Aron's wife, the twins' own mother — before she was destroyed by grief."

"Wait!" Knowing what Ileana was about to point out, Karsh stopped her. "Yes, there is every chance that Thantos forced Miranda into giving him that alibi, tricked her into saying what she did — but she is no longer able to tell her story."

"And, if Thantos has his way, he will do the same to Miranda's children!" Ileana declared. "They are Aron's true heirs. Camryn and Alexandra! With their father dead, his share of CompUmage belongs to them. And you know as well as I do," she confidently predicted, "that Thantos will sway them to his side or destroy them."

CHAPTER SEVEN
A BAD INFLUENCE

The dozen or so kids who showed up for orientation were sitting at the front of the auditorium when Alex and Madison entered. Cade Richman was sitting alone at the back.

Alex didn't notice him right away. She was halfway down the aisle, feeling overwhelmed by Madison's endless chatter.

Suddenly, a waft of soap and leather drifted toward her, making her almost dizzy with delight. She tried to pick up Cade's thoughts, but all she could hear was Madison rattling on.

"So I was, like, totally terrified. I thought, Omigosh,

this can't be happening. On my very first day at school. First day? Excuse me, first hour! And I totally never saw that toadhead before in my life. So I was like, omigosh. I'm gonna, like, totally die. Of embarrassment, I mean. And then I saw you guys. So I said, like, those girls. They're not gonna let —"

With Madison chirping nonstop at her side, Alex looked over her shoulder at Cade.

He gave her a huge smile, nothing held back.

"Madison," she said. "Save me a seat, okay? I'll catch up with you in a minute."

Alex started back up the aisle toward Cade. Madison followed, her gum-soled shoes squeaking on the wooden floor. "I mean, I just looked at you guys and I knew you wouldn't let anything bad happen to me. And omigosh, I was sooo right, right?"

"Hey," Cade said, standing slowly. "I figured if I sat back here I'd see you coming in."

Alex opened her mouth, but it was Madison's high-pitched voice that shrilled, "Oh, hi! You're the one who gave me back my wallet. I'm Madison Knudnick. The K is silent." She extended her hand — her small paw, Alex couldn't help thinking — and Cade, grinning good-naturedly, shook it.

Madison didn't take a breath or skip a beat. "Wow, I was so hoping I'd see you again. I mean, omigosh, I just wanted to say thanks, you know. But by the time I pulled myself together you were gone —"

"Good morning. Good morning, people, and welcome!" a grating voice called out. It belonged to a heavyset man in a rumpled khaki suit who had stepped out onto the stage. "You there, with the long hair, boy or girl, whatever you are, face front, please." The man's nylon shirt was too tight; it pulled across his potbelly. His tie was short and wide as a kite. His jacket fairly rattled with pens, which explained the ink stain on his pocket. "All right, let's sit down and be quiet, everyone."

Cade moved in and Alex took the seat next to him. Madison lost no time shooing them over, then plunking down into the aisle seat on the other side of Alex.

"Good morning, people. Like you, I'm new to Marble Bay High. My name is Mr. Shnorer, and some of you lucky tenth graders will get to know me better in English —"

"Guess who?" Alex whispered to Cade, showing him her class schedule.

"I've got English with someone named Woolsey," he responded softly.

"So does Cam, I think —" she said, with a quick stab of envy.

"Omigosh," Madison burst out in her screechy

squeal. "Me, too. Ms. Woolsey. Yuck. I was, like, so hoping we'd be in the same classes, Alex. I know how much it would mean to you. Getting to know me and all. Oh, wow, you must be really bummed!"

"Oh, wow, yeah. To the max." Trying to keep a straight face, Alex glanced at Cade. They had to quickly turn away from each other to keep from laughing aloud.

"Private conversation?" Mr. Shnorer called out, smiling coldly at them. He'd taken out one of his pens and was impatiently tapping it against his palm.

Alex shrunk down in her seat. Madison jumped up. "We were just saying how props it is that my friend Alex is in your class."

"Alex? Alex who?"

"Fielding," Alex mumbled.

"Excuse me?" Mr. Shnorer said, exaggeratedly cupping a hand to his ear. "A little while ago I could hear every word you said. Don't be shy now."

Most of the kids down front had turned to stare at her. A few sniggered nervously.

"Fielding," Madison piped up.

"Fielding." The English teacher narrowed his eyes, focusing in on Alex as if he was memorizing her face. "I'm sure we're all delighted to meet you, Alex Fielding. And now, with Miss Fielding's permission, of course, I'd like to continue telling those who care to listen a few things about Marble Bay High School that may make their first term here — and mine — more enjoyable."

Madison sat at last. "Wow, what an old grouch," she said, too loudly.

Alex scooched farther down in her seat. Her only comfort was that she was sitting next to Cade. As the orientation droned on, she inhaled again his sweet soapy scent, spiced with the salty tang of leather. How could she have thought he had some weird secret? He seemed so open to her now.

Mr. Shnorer might just as well have been named Snore-er, she thought. His boring voice and Cade's nearness lulled her almost to sleep. In the stuffy auditorium, she closed her eyes for a moment.

And heard:

A terrible screech of tires. Two voices, both female: one screaming in horror; the other gasping, "No!" Then, worst of all, a sickening thud.

To steady herself, to hold on to something solid, Alex grabbed for the wooden armrests of her seat. What her hands found instead were Cade's arm and Madison's — one of which sent a shock through her, an electric bristle of energy. The same sharp tingling she'd felt the first time she'd brushed Doc's sleeve. And his hand when he was the old policeman Karsh. And the uniform of his beautiful blond partner, Officer Ileana.

Alex's eyes flew open. Whose arm had given her the shock — Cade's or Madison's? Whose sleeve or hand had she accidentally touched?

She looked down at the armrests on either side of her. They were empty now. Both Cade and Madison were unenthusiastically clapping at something Mr. Shnorer had said.

That afternoon, Alex sat in class, listening again to the chunky English teacher's monotonous voice.

Dylan, who was sitting directly behind her, passed her a note. *You weren't kidding about this guy*, it said. *What a snore*.

Although Dyl was ten months younger than Camryn, Emily had wanted her children to start school together. Which was why Cam's baby brother was in the tenth grade. Hooray for Emily, Alex thought, grateful to have a friendly face in English, even if the friendly face was wearing blue streaks in his blond hair and practically everyone in class had something to say or whisper about that. Including Mr. Shnorer, of course, who'd welcomed Dylan by asking if he and "Miss Fielding" went to the same hairdresser.

The scruffy teacher was tapping one of his pens again, this time against his cheek — which irritated Alex almost as much as the fact that he wasn't actually teaching anything. He was lazily delivering a classroom version of his orientation speech. It was a double drag since, one, Alex had already suffered through the boring lecture once and, two, English was one of her favorite subjects, a class she ordinarily looked forward to.

So what do you think about Cade? she scribbled on Dylan's note and passed it back to him.

He leaned forward and whispered, "Who's Cade?"

Alex turned and rolled her eyes at him. "The guy in the leather jacket. From this morning?"

"The lock-picker?" Dylan asked.

Alex sighed. "The what? Speak English much?"

"You're talking about the dude who offered to crack your combination lock, right?"

"Forget it," Alex snapped, turning back to face front.

A pen whizzed over her head and hit the back wall behind Dylan. "Oh, my," Mr. Shnorer said, "some of these pens are so slippery."

Alex couldn't believe it. The man had thrown something at them! A few kids chuckled along with the teacher; most gasped or glared at him.

"Want to share your conversation with the class,

Alex?" He drew another pen from his pocket and began beating his palm with it.

Steaming, she shook her head.

"Stand, please," Mr. Shnorer ordered. "And do tell us what was more important than what I was saying."

Alex stood very slowly. "Almost anything," she said.

The percentage shifted. This time most of the class chuckled and only a few gasped. Unfortunately, Mr. Shnorer was one of the gaspers.

"Perhaps you and . . ." He checked his attendance sheet. "Dylan. Dylan Barnes . . . would like to finish your conversation outside?"

"Love to," Alex answered.

"You bet!" Dylan stood, too.

"All right, then." The teacher quickly pulled a sheet of paper from his desk drawer and began scrawling something on it. "Here's a pass to the principal's office. I'm sure Mrs. Hammond will give you the privacy you need. Possibly for several hours."

"We're toast," Dylan whispered. "Detention."

"Yeah, and it's only day one," Alex pointed out. "Dude, this is one advanced school. I don't usually do face time with the authorities until at least the second day of the term." She snatched the slip from Mr. Shnorer's hand, wishing she had Cam's eyeballing power. She'd have melted every pen in the goonball's pocket and fried his scuzzy see-through shirt.

Of course, there were a few tricks she could pull on her own. But she wasn't in this alone, Alex reminded herself. There was Dylan to consider — and, from the looks of it, he was not the happy puppy.

Olivia Hammond was Mr. Shnorer's exact opposite. She was handsomely fit, neat as a pin, with big, light brown eyes that reminded Alex of her mother's eyes and a stylish blunt haircut that would have looked buff on Sara. The principal accepted the note Alex handed her and asked Dylan and Alex to sit. The armchairs she indicated were comfortable and upholstered in somewhat shabby brown leather.

While Alex sat at the edge of her seat, eyes following the pacing principal, Dylan leaned back, the picture of resigned bum-osity.

Insolent? Mrs. Hammond read the note to herself. *Insolent, inattentive, insubordinate —*

"— And in trouble," Alex couldn't help adding.

"Excuse me?" The principal glanced up, startled.

"Um, I said, 'Are we in trouble?'" Alex ad-libbed.

"Yeah, like, are we going to get detention?" Dylan wanted to know.

"Well . . ." Mrs. Hammond's surprised look changed

to one of amusement. "It's a little early in the term for that, Dylan. I'm not sure we have our detention staff set up yet. Alexandra, I know that you're new to Marble Bay, and I'm sure you have a lot to contribute." She set down the note and leaned back against her desk. "Why don't you tell me what happened."

Dylan did most of the talking. Although the principal's face was set in an understanding smile, when he got to the part about Mr. Shnorer throwing a pen, Alex heard Mrs. Hammond exclaim, *Oh, no. Please tell me it was an accident*. What she said aloud was: "I see. Well, Mr. Shnorer is new to our school as well. Why don't we chalk up today's incident as first-day jitters all around?"

Dylan's bliss was brief.

"But I will have to send a note home with you and I'll need your parents' signature —"

"They're not my parents," Alex said automatically.

"So Mrs. Barnes explained," Olivia Hammond said kindly. "But it's my understanding that Mr. Barnes has set the wheels in motion for them to become your legal guardians —"

There was a brusque knock at the principal's door and, a second later, the school clerk appeared, saying in a flustered voice, "Mrs. Hammond, the police are here. They have questions about one of our students."

CHAPTER EIGHT
VOICES OF THE PAST

"Did you see them?" Cam asked after school.

"Who, the cops? Yeah," Dylan responded glumly. Skateboard tucked under his arm, he was walking Cam and Alex to the bike rack. "We had front-row seats."

Alex pinched his arm.

"Yeow," Dyl hollered. "I didn't tell her we were in Hammond's office. Why'd you do that?"

"To keep you from blabbing your guts out, but clearly my plan backfired."

"You know who they reminded me of?" Caught up in her own thoughts, Cam continued. "They reminded me of Officer Karsh and —"

"Ileana," Alex said. "What about them?"

"Well, it got me thinking again —" Cam said, unlocking her bicycle.

"Always dangerous."

"You're going straight home, right?" Dylan reminded Alex.

"I said I'd be there." Pulling her bike, formerly his bike, out of the rack, she rolled her eyes. "It was totally my fault, okay? I'll tell Emily and Dave that."

"That's not what I meant." He scowled. "Oh, forget you. I'm outta here."

"I'll be there, Dylan. I'm going right to the house. Wait for me," Alex called after him, hoping he heard her over the whoosh of his skateboard. "Dyl, don't say anything till I get there."

Well, that had gotten Cam's attention. She'd put her trip down memory lane on pause and was staring at Alex, waiting for an explanation of what was up between her and Dylan.

"Don't even ask," Alex advised. "Anyway, the cops who popped into Hammond's office today looked nothing like the dream team who showed up the night we cut Marleigh loose."

"I know. I only said they reminded me of the other ones. And because I was thinking of that, I remembered the big, bearded guy with the heavy boots, who Officer Ileana or waitress Ileana —"

"Or Ileana Barbie?" Alex teased.

"— warned us about." Cam ignored the interruption. "Anyway, monster man or whatever his real name is —"

"Thantos," Alex told her. "Weird name, right? I think I know what it means, but I'm going to check it out with Mrs. Bass."

Mrs. Bass was the Crow Creek librarian. She'd helped Alex send an e-mail to Cam on the library's computer. And now she'd set up e-mail addresses for Evan and Lucinda, Alex's best buds in Montana, so that they could keep in touch with her.

Doris Bass, Alex had told Cam, had been a friend of her mother's. She and Sara had gone to grade school together.

"Right. Thantos," Cam said now. "Alex, he said he knew our real mom, knew where she was, and that only he could take us to her —"

Alex's face turned stony. "I already know where *my* mom is," she cut Cam off. "She's dead. She died of lung cancer and I couldn't do anything to help her."

She remembered the dream she'd had the night after they'd rescued Marleigh. Doc, or Officer Karsh, came to Alex in that dream. He told her there was nothing she could have done to save her mom. It was just Sara's time, he'd said.

She guessed it had helped to believe that for a while. Just as it had helped to pretend that she was on vacation, taking a break from Crow Creek, and that when she went home Sara would still be there, alive, waiting. Only reality kept rearing its ugly head.

Reality. Definition: Sara, the only mother Alex had ever known, the only one she'd ever wanted, was gone for good.

"You want to know why?" Alex asked Cam, without looking at her. Her voice broke unexpectedly. She cleared her throat, embarrassed, almost angry. "She died because we were broke. Big-time. Massively. Without dollar one. We were . . . I mean, my moms was . . . *literally* dead broke."

"Als, I'm sorry," Cam began.

But Alex climbed on the dirt bike that had belonged to Dylan and started peddling toward the house, as she'd promised him she would.

On her sleek red racer, Cam rode after her. "Alex, wait up. I'm sorry."

"Know why we were broke?" Alex called over her shoulder, not caring that other kids were leaving school, moving in herds, milling at the oh-so-quaint stone benches of Money Bags High, which they happened to be biking past. "Because my loser dad left us with nothing but his dumb debts!"

The sight of Kristen and Bree in their designer duds, waiting at the curb for Bree's housekeeper to pick them up, just egged Alex on. "And like a minute after my so-called father was smoke, a hundred creeps crawled out of the woodwork demanding that my *moms* come up with the Benjis he supposedly scammed off them," she went on, loud enough for the Galleria girls to hear.

Out of the corner of her eye, she saw, with sick satisfaction, their shocked exchange of looks. "End of convo, Cam. You want to find your real mother, you go, Sherlock. But Sara Fielding was mine."

Dylan was in the driveway, fiddling with the trucks on his skateboard, when first Alex, then Cam rode up. "Okay, let's do this thing," Alex grumbled, dropping the dirt bike against the garage wall.

"What's going on?" Cam asked, dismounting. "I'm going to find out anyway. Maybe I can help —"

"We got sent to Hammond's office," Dylan told her, following Alex into the house.

Cam shook her head and took off after them. "For what?"

"For mouthing off at this barrel-bellied Barney who gets his kicks embarrassing kids and hurling pens —"

"Shnorer," Alex reported.

"The new English Lit guy?" Cam asked, aghast.

"Don't lose your lunch over it," Alex advised. "I didn't do anything . . . you know, *serious* to him. The man is beyond snarky. In fact, I wouldn't be surprised if he was —"

"Not even!" Cam gasped, knowing what Alex was thinking. "The messenger?"

"Messenger? I wish," Dylan said, imagining Shnorer on a bike, with a big old canvas sack, filled with packages and oversize envelopes, slung across his chest. "He's a teacher. And Mom is going to bust a gut —"

"Oh, really?" Emily glanced over her shoulder as they entered the kitchen. She was at her desk, shuffling through fabric swatches, a blueprint of her client's living room spread out before her. Smiling, she swiveled to face them. "What am I going to bust a gut about?"

Alex and Cam looked at each other. *Don't make a joke about it*, Cam silently begged. *Thanks for the tip*, Alex responded sarcastically, then crossed the floor and handed Emily Mrs. Hammond's note. "Houston, we have a problem," she quipped. Behind her she could hear Cam groaning.

"Mom, listen —" Dylan began.

Emily held up her hand to hush him while she read. When she looked up, her smile was gone, and so was most of the color in her face. "If you're going to start giving me excuses for this, don't bother," she warned Dylan.

"That's not what I was going to do." He ran a hand through his choppy two-tone 'do — which Alex wished he hadn't, since it only called attention to his last offense, the blue-streak caper, which Emily was sure Alex had talked him into. "I was going to say he deserved it. The guy's a real —"

"Don't say it!" his mother commanded. "And you, Alexandra . . ." Emily's blue eyes went cold. She stood abruptly and shook Mrs. Hammond's letter at Alex. "I expected more of you. Although I don't know why. I just thought you'd appreciate —" She stopped brusquely and tossed the note down onto her desk. "I'll sign this slip and so will your father —"

"Right," Alex said. "Be sure to let me know when you dig him up." She turned on her heels and headed out of the room.

Cam started after her. "You stay right here," her mother commanded. "I want to talk to you. And I think your father will, too."

Dave strode into the kitchen, as if on cue.

"Whasssssup?" he teased. But after taking in the glum scene, he quickly switched gears. He dropped his briefcase onto a chair and drew his Ben Franklin–style bifocals from their perch on top of his head down onto the bridge of his nose. This last gesture was a sign that he was ready for business. "Okay. What's going on?" he said, with a touch of wariness.

Cam climbed the stairs in a foul mood. Her father wanted her to baby-sit Alex. "Poor Alex," he'd called her, after Emily finished reading Dylan the riot act and then stomped after him out of the kitchen. "Just keep an eye out for her, Cami," he'd said. "Poor kid, she's new here and she's been through so much —"

"Oh, like I haven't gone through anything, right?" Cam had grumbled. "Only finding out, fourteen years after the fact, that I was adopted and had an identical twin I'd never met!"

And there was plenty more she'd been through that she wasn't about to discuss with David, the make-believe dad.

Like how she knew things before they happened.

And saw things no one else could see.

And could talk to Alex without words and sometimes hear what her newfound, trouble-prone twin was thinking.

And discovered that her eyes could be fire hazards. That, like the sun, they could dazzle and blind, or pin a person with a ray of lethal light.

Oh, yeah, and how about, after a lifetime of being the only gray-eyed girl she knew, the only one with her exact, almost metallic, gold-flecked, black-rimmed gray eyes, she'd was suddenly running into a regular rash of gray-eyed babes: Alex, of course, and Ileana.

Cam was miffed, bummed, and so not into being the "mature" twin saddled with the job of looking after the wayward, wild girl of the West.

Like Alex cared? Look at her, Cam thought, after opening the door to their room. The whole Barnes household was stressed to the max, and there was Alexandra the Great, sitting cross-legged on her bed, scrounging through the sorry wad of junk jewelry that Doc had packed for her before bringing her to Marble Bay.

And Cam's computer was on, too. It wasn't like "Poor Alex" had been sitting around feeling rotten about messing up at school and at home. Or about taking Dylan down with her — although, Cam had to admit, her skateboarding, earring-wearing, formerly longhaired blond bro didn't need much help in that department.

"Thanks for the vote of confidence," Alex said without looking up.

"Excuse me?" Cam asked coldly. "I assume you trespassed on my thoughts again. Which part of what I was thinking did you mistake for a vote of confidence?"

"My, aren't we frosty? I was referring to your brilliant insight that your brother is capable of screwing up without my leadership skills."

"Stay out," Cam said. "Just mind your own business and stay out of my mind, okay?"

"Don't I wish I could." Alex picked a faded pink box out of the trinket trash on the bed. She opened it, peered in, and then quickly snapped it shut again. "It's not my fault that I hear way more of your boring beliefs than I want to." Getting up abruptly, she took the silk-covered box with her into their bathroom and slammed the door.

Inside the old box was the necklace Doc had said belonged to her mother. Without turning on the bathroom light, Alex carefully took out the delicate necklace and carried it to the window. Sadly, lovingly, she studied the moon charm in the thin glow of the fading day.

In their bedroom, mindlessly toying with her own necklace, Cam listened raptly, wondering if she could see through the door, pierce it with her intense gaze. No, she decided, even if she could, she wouldn't. Some people had a conscience about how they used their mojo.

Instead, she wandered over to the computer to check her e-mail. What she saw on the screen was the beginning of a note from Alex to Mrs. Bass at the Crow Creek library. *Do you know what Thantos means? It reminds me of something I read in that mythology book I brought back way overdue when Mom —*

The message ended there. Ended on the word *Mom*.

Without wanting to or trying to, Cam knew what had happened. In the middle of e-mailing the librarian, Alex had remembered her mother — their mother. . . . She'd probably felt the urge to hold on to something that had belonged to or been worn by Sara. Something Alex kept in that old jewelry stash —

Cam felt so locked out. She longed to know more about Sara. All she'd been able to pry from Alex so far was that their mother was strong, loving, and had brown, not gray eyes. Oh, yeah, and that she and the Crow Creek librarian had gone to school together.

But if Sara, who had died just weeks ago, was their mother, then who was it the madman, the murderer, Thantos, said he could take them to? Cam shivered as the thought occurred to her that it was Sara he was talking about, that he could take them to meet a dead person.

Yet what if Sara was not their real mom? What if Alex, like Cam herself, had been duped? What if the woman Alex had called mom for fourteen years was no more her true biological mother than Emily was Cam's?

Camryn looked up at the PC monitor again. And saw: *Dbass@Crowcreek.lib*.

A familiar feeling shook her. Shoulders hunched,

she hugged herself and trembled. It was what Beth called her "hunch hunch."

Why hadn't she thought of it before, she wondered, smiling. Alex didn't want to talk about Sara — but maybe Doris Bass would.

"Stay out of your mind, but it's okay for you to break into my e-mails?" Alex accused a few minutes later when she came out of the bathroom.

"How embarrassed am I that I read two whole sentences on a subject you already discussed with me? Hello. Not very. Or did you forget you told me you were going to ask Library Lady about the creep's name?"

"Oh, I'm so sorry," Alex responded sarcastically. "I guess you just had an irresistible urge to chill in the computer chair and stare at the screen."

"I've got better things to do," Cam said. "Like making up an invite for the Halloween sleepover I'm going to throw."

"Halloween's my birthday," Alex said without thinking. Her hand, the one in which she grasped her mother's necklace, was growing warm.

"Duh. What a coincidence. It's mine, too."

Alex walked over to the computer and glanced at the monitor. There was a bright orange pumpkin on the screen. Then, with a click of the mouse, the silhouette of a witch on a flying broomstick appeared.

"Cool," Alex wanted to say, but the word "hot" left her lips. The gold charm was searing her palm. She opened her fingers and stared at the graceful half-moon.

"Hot? Well, I wouldn't go that far." Cam laughed and swiveled around on her computer chair. "Als, what's wrong?"

Alex's face was flushed and frightened. Her hand seemed to be moving on its own toward her twin's throat. She couldn't pull it back. Worse than that, she didn't want to.

Cam stood, took a step back, then realized that the charm in Alex's open hand looked like a mirror image of the one dangling from her own necklace. She lifted her shimmering chain to check out the similarity.

Before it totally registered that her pendant had rays like the sun, while Alex's looked more like a half-moon, Cam could feel the chain straining against the back of her neck. She could feel her charm pulling toward Alex's.

With a sudden surge, they connected.

Alex's half-moon and Cam's radiant sun linked with a bang!

Together they formed a perfect circle.

All at once, soft voices filled the room.

Aron, they're beautiful.

I made them, a man's voice responded. *This one's for you, Miranda. These are for our daughters.*

With great effort, gritting her teeth to keep from grunting, Alex pulled back her hand. The bond that linked the necklaces was broken. The voices stopped, as both girls were thrown backward. Alex landed on her back on the bed. Cam fell into her computer chair, which wheeled wildly across the floor, until it crashed against the wall.

Trembling, they looked around the room. "Who was that? Who said that?" Cam asked in a hushed voice. But she thought she knew.

With a solemn, sinking heart, because the woman's voice had not been Sara's, Alex had the same idea.

But was it possible? Had they heard the voices of their true parents?

Alex couldn't accept that, didn't want to believe it. "Who said what?" she responded, turning her back on Camryn.

"Als," Cam pressed, "I think I heard our parents. Did Sara have a soft voice and, don't think I'm crazy, but did she smell like pine trees and baby powder?"

Alex couldn't help herself. "No," she admitted, staring down at the charm Doc had given her. "My moms smelled like violets. They were her favorite flower." She saw drops splash onto the golden moon in her palm and realized that she was crying.

Cam's fingers, identical to Alex's but for the nails — Alex's bitten and painted blue; Cam's neatly polished with clear gloss — came into view. Gently, they lifted the necklace from Alex's hand and fastened it around her neck.

She might just as well have fastened their veins together. Wearing their birth necklaces, one pulse beat between them, strong and demanding.

They clutched each other's hands, feeling the strange surge of power racing through them.

Alex looked up. She stared directly into her sister's eyes, which were now as misty as her own.

"Als, I think it was them," Cam said.

The afternoon, which had been mild for autumn, turned suddenly stormy. Wind set the trees creaking. Branches tapped at their windows. There was a lonely howling outside, broken by a crackling spear of lightning. Somewhere a loose shutter banged against the house.

Alex and Cam stood in the center of the room, holding on to each other. The noise and chaos around them was fierce, but they were surprisingly unafraid.

CHAPTER NINE
THE TRUTH ABOUT CADE

"Could you, like, *be* less enthusiastic to see me?" Bree asked. Gathered in a high ponytail, a shock of blond-highlighted hair erupted from the top of her head. The 'do reminded Cam of Wilma Flintstone and Alex of Old Faithful. "I mean, like who were you expecting, Ben . . . Brad . . . Brice?"

"Probably me," Dylan cracked, following Bree into the twins' room. She had changed from her Alloy skirt and sweater outfit to an after-school ensemble of crop top and clam-diggers. "Wait till you hear Banana's latest scoop."

Bree tried to glower at the boy but couldn't. She

was too psyched. Her green eyes glistened happily with dish.

Cam's heart sank. She and Alex had seemed so close to a connection with their parents. "Oh, hey. Hi, Bree."

"Okay. Well, later." Alex tried to pull away from Cam.

"But Alexandra —" Bree pretended to pout. "You'll miss the dirt of the decade. And it's all about that IP who's so crushed on you."

"IP?" Alex drew a blank.

"Improvement project," Cam translated. "She means . . . Cade, right?" she asked, hanging on to Alex's hand.

"Bree says leather boy is loaded," Dylan spilled the beans. "His 'rents bought that awesome sick mansion in the Heights —"

"See if I ever give you firsties on a hot headline again!" Bree pouted for real. "Before Dyl-erious blurts the best part, guess why the police were at school today?"

"Obviously, it has something to do with Cade," Cam said impatiently.

"Go, mojo girl," Bree teased. "Seems there's been a series of B and E's at Chateau Richman —"

"B and E? What's that short for," Dylan asked mischievously, "Bree and Eddie?"

Alex and Cam looked at each other. Was baby bro

getting in touch with his mojo side, Cam wondered, because Eddie was who she was just thinking about.

How did Dylan know that? And, more important, how had Eddie Robins known that Cade was rich when no one else at school seemed to get it — certainly not by the way the new guy dressed and acted.

Good question, Alex agreed, tuning into her double's thoughts to discover they were the same as her own. "Let's ask Eddie," she said aloud.

Cam's free hand found her sun charm. It was warm. A faint buzzing tickled her fingertips when she touched it. It had never felt like that before.

Then again, it had never moved as it did minutes ago, never sought and found its missing half.

She glanced at Alex and saw, with wonder, that her twin was doing the exact same thing, resting her fingers lightly on her moon charm.

Cam's sight began to blur. The low-voltage tingle she'd felt in her fingertips had become a ripple of energy that passed through their clasped hands. Cam felt herself growing dizzy. Again, she heard the squeal of tires, screeching laughter, and then a bloodcurdling thud.

"Yeeow!" Alex freed her hand from Cam's suddenly crushing grasp. "What's up with you? I'd say, 'Get a grip,' but you so already have!"

"I saw it again," Cam whispered.

"I know," Alex responded softly. "I heard it. There was a crash. And then a scream —"

Dylan was checking them out, trying to hear what they were saying. Bree, however, was a few beats back and oblivious. "Ask him?" she cried indignantly. "You can't think that bald Barney and I have anything in common!"

It took a moment for Cam and Alex to realize that she was talking about Eddie.

"B and E is cop-speak for Breaking and Entering," Brianna instructed. "As in: Someone's been breaking and entering Cade's casa, and leaving with sacks of Benjis."

"Money," Cam agreed. "Lots and lots of it."

Ask Eddie. Find out why he called Cade "Richie Rich Kid" and how he knew Cade's father made "big bucks." That was their mission.

It was also a way to duck out of dealing with what had happened before Bree and Dylan showed up.

Alex didn't want to talk about their weird necklaces or the spooky voices they'd both heard. Maybe Cam was right. Maybe the voices did belong to their "real" parents. If it was true, Alex wasn't ready to face it. She didn't want to find out that the mother she'd loved and lost had been just as dishonest as Emily and Dave.

Cam was just as willing to drop the touchy subject. For now.

Following her hunch that Doris Bass knew more about Alex's mother and missing father than Alex herself did, Cam waited until Alex was asleep and e-mailed the Crow Creek librarian asking for her help. Until she had an answer, she'd just as soon avoid arguing with Alex about who their parents were.

So they were both relieved to focus on unraveling the Eddie-Cade connection. But the bully didn't show up for school the next day. Not until Friday did they get their chance.

Marble Bay High School was still humming with guesses and rumors about what the police were doing there earlier in the week. Like salsa, theories ranged from mild to spicy. Bree's scoop was among the hottest. Her exposé of the mysterious robberies at Cade Richman's "castle" had drawn a crowd of gossip groupies.

Moving past Bree's audience to their own lockers, Cam and Alex spotted Edgar Robins plowing down the hall. Alone. Caught up in his own thoughts, the bully was mindlessly elbowing people out of his path. Cam had never seen him looking so grim and hassled.

"What luck. There's our boy." Alex tossed her afternoon gear — gym clothes, science syllabus, and math books — into her locker.

"Maybe we should interview him another time," Cam suggested. "He so does not look Barbara Walters–ready."

"We'll just ask how come he knew Cade was rich. One quick question —"

"Yo, yo, dude-esses. S'up?" Dylan caught up with the twins and peeled off from his grungy gang — all of them in low-slung baggies, XL T-shirts, and ridiculously huge unlaced high-tops. They also sported earrings, eye rings, nose rings, lip rings, tongue rings, and a rainbow of hair colors — though only Dylan's was striped neon blue.

Which, for some reason, caught Eddie's eye and seemed to offend him. "Dyl-pickle," he called out as soon as the rest of Dylan's crew had disappeared around a corner. "Who puked in your hair?"

Dylan took a step forward. Cam looked down and sighed. Alex shook her head at Eddie and said sadly, "Your learning curve must be a complete circle."

"Huh?" the hulk replied, his brow dipping lower over his little pig eyes. "You wanna start something, double trouble?" Surprised and pleased by his sudden surge of wit, he added, "Ha-ha-ha."

Alex and Cam rolled their eyes at the same time.

"Hey, Pistachio's blue period —" Eddie said to Alex.

"Pistachio?" Cam echoed, perplexed.

"He means Picasso," Dylan translated.

Eddie ignored him and continued sneering at Alex.

"Where's that butt-ugly skull you were wearin'? Where'd you get that new, dumb thing?"

Automatically, Alex grasped her half-moon charm. It seemed to be heating up again. Cam's hands flew to her sun charm. Eddie caught the motion. With a mean gleam in his eye, his hand shot out, intent on snatching Cam's necklace.

She spun out of his reach and he cried out in agony, blisters welling up on his fingers.

"Yo, wha — ?!" Dylan gulped.

Go, you fire girl, Alex silently congratulated Cam. *You stir-fried the porker.*

Whew. Major hex, Als! Cam said at the same time. *That is so the spell I'd like to learn.*

"Excuse me?" they said together. "You mean you didn't . . . ?" They both stopped and stared at each other's necklace.

It's the charms, Cam guessed. *Mine's heating up again. What about yours?*

Simmering, Alex agreed. *Is it 'cause we're wearing them together?*

Cam had no time to answer. Eddie's flames had gone out and he was lunging at her.

Dylan jumped between them, his fist cocked. Before he could fully connect, Eddie broke into a spastic dance. The bristly headed boy's legs flailed and twisted. "I'm burning up!" he shouted. His arms made weird circles in the air, as if he were trying to keep himself from falling backward.

"Yo, I barely laid a glove on him," Dylan explained to a group of bug-eyed kids who'd heard the commotion.

"O.M.G.!" With one hand still clutching her overheated charm, Cam whispered, "Alex, you'll never believe this. I did it! I mean, I sort of wished it."

"I totally believe you. Too bad he wasn't holding a ball," Alex mused, wistfully recalling the time she'd gotten a trash-talking girl bully to bean herself with a basketball. That was when Alex discovered she could make stuff move just by thinking about it. Now she tapped her chewed-up nails against her half-moon necklace, then smiled as, out of nowhere, she pictured Eddie lying helpless on his back, limbs tangled uselessly.

A second later she heard him flop like a sack of raw dough onto the green linoleum tiles of the corridor. Gasps and giggles rippled through the gathered crowd.

"I didn't do it." Dylan scanned the mob for witnesses, while Alex and Cam knelt beside the thrashing bully.

"Don't touch me." Eddie cringed. "What are you, witches?"

"T'Witches," Cam whispered impishly.

"Twins. Witches. Get it?" Alex laughed. "We're T'Witches. Which means we can unpretzel you — for a price."

"That ain't fair," Eddie growled. "I got no money. I don't even get no allowance anymore."

"Okay, then just answer a question. How did you know that Cade's family was rich?"

"My old man, he's a landscaper. He works at the Richman house, up there in the Heights. Couple of times this summer, I went along to help him out. They've got money, okay, but I wouldn't trade with them, no way," he asserted. "Like, Cade's got this sister — she's a mess, popping Prozac and crying all the time. She was supposed to be in summer school, but she came back early, had a nervous breakdown or something —"

"Oh, no. Not again, not now." Cam's eyes had begun to tear. She pressed her hands against her throbbing temples.

A second later, Alex whispered, "I know. The car. The crash. I heard it again, too."

Eddie tried to sit up. And failed. "That's it. That's all I know," he said, trying to keep his voice down. "'N' I don't care what you are. Witches, whatever. I told you what you wanted. Now undo me!"

Alex and Cam exchanged nervous glances.

"You're kiddin' me, right?" Eddie panicked. "You knew how to get me into this WWF hold, but now you don't know how to get me out?!"

"And we thought he was stupid," Alex said.

CHAPTER TEN
AN ARREST AT SCHOOL

The crowd parted suddenly. Kids started backing away. "All right, boys and girls, let's all get to our classes now. No one wants to be late." Alex recognized Mr. Shnorer's irritating, high-pitched voice. "People, what's going on here?"

"Nothing," Dylan blurted. "Nothing's going on —"

"Barnes? You again?"

True to his promise not to rat out Cam or Alex, Eddie pointed his chin — one of his few still-movable parts — at Cam's brother. "He hit me!" the twisted bully hollered.

"Oh, baloney!" Alex and Cam heard Madison squeak before they could see her. "Yeah, right, like Camryn

Barnes's brother would even touch you. Oh, boy, what a liar."

The scrawny girl pushed her way to the front. "Oh, wow. Like, how long can your nose grow? Mr. Shnorer, that's the boy who tried to steal my wallet yesterday."

"You. Get up," Shnorer ordered Eddie.

"I can't!" the bully raged.

"Liar, liar, pants on fire," Madison chanted. She was wearing a fluffy white sweater in which she looked far more like a guinea pig than a rat.

"Shut up! You blind or something?! Just look." Eddie pointed to his legs — then realized, just as Alex and Cam did, that he could move his arms, that they'd somehow unlocked. He looked at his feet. They were still twisted into a position that qualified him for *Ripley's Believe It or Not.*

But he could wriggle his toes. And then flex his ankles. And finally, straighten his legs. "Thanks," he whispered to Alex and Cam, and scrambled to his feet.

The twins looked at each other, stumped.

Neither of them had set the boy free. They turned to stare suspiciously — Alex at Mr. Shnorer, who was hauling Eddie and Dylan to the principal's office, and Cam at Madison, who was grinning a triumphant, hamster grin.

The homeroom bell rang and kids were suddenly

dashing off in all directions. "I'm going to try to bail Dylan out," Cam told Alex. "We'll . . . talk later."

"Deal," Alex agreed, taking off down the other end of the hall.

"Alexandra, Alexandra!" Madison came bustling after her. "Are you going to team tryouts this afternoon?"

"I don't think so," Alex said over her shoulder, then rounded the corner and crashed into Cade.

"Guess you aced your fitness test." He held her at arm's length and laughed.

"Huh?" was Alex's brilliant response.

"You know. They check you out in the gym," the dark-haired babe explained. "See how far and fast you can go on the treadmill before you fade. Monitor your blood pressure. I'm scheduled for today, last period."

"Oh." She came back to her senses as best she could, considering Cade's nearness and the delicious aroma of soap and old leather drifting from him. "Cam and I did it yesterday —"

"You must have passed with flying colors," he teased.

"Oh, please, Alexandra. Say yes. Please, please, please." Madison caught up with them. "I'm going out for volleyball," she squeaked, looking up at Cade. "But there's basketball, softball, soccer —"

"Soccer's Cam's sport," Alex said.

"Oooo, then do volleyball with me. Please, please, please. I'll be your best friend."

"Tempting as that offer is —" Alex began.

"That'd be cool," Cade cut in. "Then I'd get to see you at the gym. I mean, if you're trying out for a team, and I'm there taking my fitness test. Catch you last period, okay?"

"It's a date," Alex agreed.

"Hooray!" Madison squealed, jumping up and down between them.

The rest of the day passed slowly for Alex. Dylan showed up for English grumbling about Mr. Shnorer. Luckily, Mrs. Hammond was out of the school for the morning so he and Eddie were scheduled to see her later in the day. By then, Dylan figured, he could round up enough kids who'd seen what had happened to prove he hadn't done anything wrong.

During class, Alex studied Mr. Shnorer, worked so hard at reading his mind that she wound up with a killer headache. All she got out of the tawdry teacher were a bunch of questions like, *What am I doing here?* and *Why me?* And, reacting to students' wrong answers, he'd silently ranted, *Think, you toad! It's a metaphor, moron, metaphor!*

Once, Alex caught him looking at her and heard

him decide, *That one is trouble*. None of which helped her figure out whether the bozo was Thantos's evil messenger. Definitely not, if she was supposed to feel drawn to him.

Madison was waiting outside math, Alex's last subject before the tryouts. "Ooo, I am so majorly psyched. Aren't you?" the quivering girl gushed, taking three little steps for every one of Alex's and still not quite keeping up with her. "That we'll be on the same team all term. And with your mojo, we'll totally win every game. And if you showed me how you do it, then, in case you got sick or whatever, I could, like, mojo for you. Then Marble Bay would never lose and everybody'd know that I was tight with the twins."

"Cam's the mojo-meister." Alex snuck a sentence in sideways, then spotted Cam and Beth coming toward them.

"Camryn! Camryn!" Madison screeched as if she'd found her long-lost best friend.

Cam gave Alex a questioning look. Alex shrugged. "You going out for soccer again?" she asked her sister.

"I guess," Cam said vaguely. "I've just got to . . . um, stop by the computer lab first."

"And then she's going to get back on that horse and ride," Beth teased.

"Horse? Oooo, you mean Camryn's going to play

soccer again, even if she did choke last season and blow the championship for Marble Bay. I heard." Madison clutched her heart in sympathy. "You had, like, a major mojo glitch, right, Camryn? Zoned in the clutch. Tanked totally. Blew the big one —"

Cam's perfect complexion was growing mottled, Alex noticed, and her gray eyes were practically smokin'. Another minute and Madison would be toast. Literally.

"How does that mojo thing work anyway?" she nattered on. "I mean, can you make it happen whenever you want? Whoops. I guess not. Otherwise that'd mean you wanted to lose the game. I guess it's kinda — like what? — out of your control and all?"

Beth was staring at the new girl, horrified. "You'd better see your veterinarian," she advised. "Hoof in mouth disease can be fatal."

"What fun," Cam told Alex. "We've got to do this again sometime."

"Yeah, like . . ." Beth took Cam's arm and led her away. Over her shoulder she called, "Nevuh!"

Madison looked genuinely surprised. "What's wrong with Camryn?" she asked.

It would have been funny if it hadn't been furiously annoying.

There was Cade, sitting in the stands, waiting to be

called for his fitness test. He was beaming at Alex. Every time she mashed a ball over the net, he gave her a thumbs-up.

And there was Madison, on the other side of the volleyball net, chirping nonstop in her piercing, breathless way. She'd seen Alex's half-moon pendant when they'd changed into gym clothes in the locker room. Now she wanted to know:

Where had Alex gotten that totally to-die-for necklace? Like, what happened to the punked-out skull she'd worn yesterday? Didn't Cam have a necklace just like — well, almost just like — Alex's? How choice — twins with matching necklaces. Did they have, like, a special meaning? Did they have anything to do with Cam's mojo? What was mojo anyway?

"I mean," the small but surprisingly powerful player persisted, "is it like magic? Like real witchy stuff or just, you know, a feeling?"

Alex wished Madison would shut up.

No such luck.

"Do you think mojo would work in volleyball? Or is it just a soccer thing?"

The ball was passed to Alex.

She set it up for the tall girl next to her at the net.

Who spiked it over with all her might.

Right onto Madison's head.

Madison's legs went all rubbery. Her dark eyes crossed. She sank to the floor.

Oh, no, Alex thought. *I didn't mean for that to happen.*

Oh, yes, you did, a man's voice angrily charged.

Alex stared at the fallen girl. The echo in the vast gym had made it seem as if the accusation had come from Madison — who was frowning up at her, looking extremely peeved. Others on Madison's side of the net rushed to her aid.

Alex looked over at the bleachers. Cade was no longer there. Nor was anyone who could have spoken those words. She looked around and found him. He was standing with his back to the volleyball court, waiting in front of the coach's table to fill out a form for his fitness test.

Alex ducked under the net and put out her hand to help Madison, but the girl refused her aid. Then, clearly feeling wobbly again, she leaned against Alex to steady herself.

And there was the buzz. The funny electric tickle that Alex had felt the first time she brushed against Doc's sleeve. She stared hard at Madison, half expecting to find Doc's bony white face lurking beneath Madison's flushed features.

"Did you feel that?" the small girl asked.

"What?" Alex challenged.

"A shock. It's been happening all day. Between the new shampoo I used and this dumb sweater, I'm, like, all staticky."

The second of three volleyball tryout games was just ending when Dylan ran into the gym. Spotting Alex, he paced impatiently on the sidelines until the game was over, then he dashed onto the court. "Eddie just got picked up by the police. They think he's the one who did it."

"Did what?" Alex glanced at the bleachers. Cade was back. He waved to her.

"Did the breaking-and-entering thing. Robbed the Richman house —"

"Oh, wow!" Madison was instantly at Alex's side. "Cade's house . . ." The gym door swung open. "Oh, hi, Camryn. Camryn, did you hear? the hyper teen shrieked as Cam entered, trailed by Beth.

"They think Eddie did all the robberies," Alex told her twin.

Cam seemed happy to hear it. Too happy. "Beth told me," she acknowledged, grinning.

"What's up with you?" Alex wanted to know. "If I said they were going to give him twenty to life, would you, like, bust out laughing?"

"No. It's just . . . I got an e-mail I've been waiting for." She didn't say, didn't even dare think: *from Doris Bass, who said she'd try to help in any way she could.* The librarian had suggested that Cam send her a list of questions. Which Cam had immediately done.

"An e-mail? You are way too easy to please," Alex noted.

"I was in the office," Beth jumped in, "getting my schedule changed. I heard them talking to Mrs. Hammond, the policemen. The same ones who showed up before. They've got footprints that match Eddie's, muddy sneaker treads inside the house —"

"It was beyond weird," Dylan said. "Eddie was, like, radically flipped. Yelling and warning them they'd better not bother his dad about it! He was out of control. Swearing at the cops and all. He says he's gonna sue them 'cause he didn't rob the place —"

"He didn't," Cam said very softly.

No one seemed to have heard her but Alex, who was about to ask whether she'd had another one of her premonitions, when Cade ambled over.

"Hey, what's up?" he asked.

"Oooo, you don't know? Your house. The robberies and whatever. Edgar Robins did it." Madison's eyes sparkled with excitement. "Only Camryn doesn't think so, right, Camryn?"

Everyone turned toward Cam, except for Alex, who was studying Madison's feral little face.

"Is that true? You don't think Eddie did it?" Dylan asked his sister.

"But why?" Beth demanded. "I mean, I told you what the police said. How come you don't believe them?"

Cam was staring oddly at Madison. "How do you know what I think?" she asked.

Madison shrugged. "I heard you. I've got excellent hearing," she claimed. "I'm right, aren't I?"

"Cami," Beth whined. "How do you know?"

"Because he doesn't drive," Cam blurted involuntarily.

"Non sequitur alert. Earth to Camryn. Help me here, Als," Dylan laughed, turning to Alex.

Alex's eyes were half closed and her head thrown back slightly, as though she was concentrating, listening. "The car crash," she whispered, out of the blue. "It was a kid. A little boy, I think —"

"Excuse me, are we interrupting another private Roswell moment?" Beth was trying for humor. It didn't really work. She was plainly feeling left out again.

Cade clasped Alex's shoulders. "What are you talking about?" he asked. "What about a car crash? A kid?" Then, embarrassed, he released her.

Madison scurried over and began to fill Cade in on Eddie's arrest.

"You don't seem thrilled that your mysterious housebreaker has been caught," Cam commented.

"I . . . I never expected this," Cade said carefully. *Everything's going wrong.*

"What went wrong?" Alex asked.

Cade stared hard at her. "Nothing. What are you talking about?"

"But didn't you just say —"

Cam knew what had happened. She cleared her throat loudly and stared meaningfully at her twin. And Alex realized that she'd finally broken through. She'd read Cade's thoughts.

CHAPTER ELEVEN
THE CLIENT

"It's him," Camryn said as they walked their bikes up the driveway. "Look at the whack way he acted when he found out Eddie was the thief —"

"NW," Alex insisted. "If anything, it's her. Talk about whack "

"You don't want to believe it just because you're crushed on him." Cam followed Alex into the garage.

"Oh, like, I'm so superficial and you're so deep? I don't think so."

Something moved in the back of the garage, startling Alex. Coming from sunlight into the shadows, she couldn't make out what it was. But she thought she heard a recognizable voice, distant, aged, and raspy. Goose bumps prickled the back of her neck. "Doc?" she whispered.

"Wrong again." Cam's eyesight, as sharp as Alex's hearing, had become even keener now that they were both wearing their necklaces. "It's only Dylan," she gloated.

He was sitting in the dark, in an old armchair Dave was supposed to be repairing. "Only Dylan?" he grumbled, standing up and unfolding the note he'd been toying with. "Thanks for the ego boost. Mom just went ballistic on me. I got another slip for her to sign, from Hammond. Thanks to Mr. Shnor-rat."

"Why didn't you take it to Dad?" Cam asked. "He's way easier —"

"'Cause he's having this major do-not-disturb session in the den," Dylan answered. "Some hotshot client —"

"Well, thanks for warming Mom up for us," Cam said, walking into the house. "Couldn't you have waited till Sunday night? I was hoping for a decent weekend."

"You?" Alex followed her twin inside. "Cade's going to call me tomorrow. He practically said so. As you would put it, he is so the mega-babe."

"Mega-babe or monster man?" Cam chided, heading for the front hall. "If he delivers a message, don't forget to share it." She started up the stairs.

"Dream on," Alex called after her. "There is nothing about Cade Richman I'm going to share with you."

"My goodness." Emily was on her way down. "Where are you going in such a hurry?"

"Hey, Mom. Gotta check my e-mail. BRB," Cam promised.

Emily shook her head.

"Be right back," Alex translated for her.

"Oh," Emily said stiffly.

"Right." Alex rolled her eyes. "Gee, I wonder if you're thinking Dylan's latest bust is my fault?"

Emily was, of course. Alex heard her thoughts as distinctly as if she'd shouted them. Emily knew she was probably being unfair, *but this strange girl* — Alex bristled at the label — this intruder, who looked exactly like her daughter but was *really so different from Cam, so rebellious and antisocial and . . .*

Emily became aware of Alex's gaze. And her inner monologue changed.

Behind the scowling defiance, Alex heard the woman tell herself, *there is sadness in those startling gray eyes*. Ha! Alex thought. *Sadness, loneliness, grief.*

Emily Barnes, she scolded herself, *this girl, this heartbroken child, has just become an orphan. She has lost the most precious human being in the world to her. Her mother . . .*

Alex had had enough. The phone rang. She ran into the kitchen to answer it. By the time Emily came into the room, Alex was sitting on top of the kitchen counter — *Why couldn't she have sat in a chair like a normal person?* — curling the phone cord around her fingers.

She grinned at Emily suddenly, then winked, melting away the last of Emily's reserve.

"Who was that?" she asked pleasantly as Alex got off the phone.

"Cade!" Alex answered. "Cade Richman from school. He asked me out! I'm going to meet him tomorrow —"

Emily sighed deeply. "I'm afraid not," she said.

"Oh, no! I don't believe this!" Alex ranted. "This is so whack. How can you do this to me? You can't. You have no right to. You're not my mother! You're no one's mother!"

"Yo, cut it out, Alex. That really stinks." It was Dylan. He was at the kitchen door.

"She's so unfair. You hate me! I bet Dave would let me go."

"I doubt that," Emily said. "It was his idea to begin with. Dylan, where's your sister? Will you find her, please?" she asked her son, who was flushed with embarrassment at the way Alex was carrying on.

He stepped out into the hallway and saw Cam charging down the stairs. "Where've you been?"

"On the Web," she answered breathlessly. "Where's Alex? I've got something to tell her."

"Not right now," Dylan cautioned. "She's in there, going a few rounds with Mom. It's not a pretty sight."

"We're not supposed to go out with anyone unless the FBI — the Federal Barnes Investigation — checks them out first!" Alex hollered as Cam entered the kitchen. "You try to reason with her. She's *your* make-believe mom!"

"Don't talk to my mother that way," Cam ordered.

"Oh, now she's your mom." Dylan got into it. "I thought Alex's mom was supposed to be your mom —"

Cam looked helplessly at Alex. *Als,* she said silently, *she's not your mom.*

"You can say that again!" Alex shouted. "And she never will be!"

Dave Barnes joined the fray. His dark curls were churned up, corkscrewing from his head, as they only did when he'd been anxiously running his hand through his hair. Whipping off his glasses, he demanded, "What's going on in here?"

Emily began to answer, but Alex jumped in. "I met

this really nice guy at school and Emily won't let me go out with him. I mean, not even in bright daylight."

"Do we know him?" Dave put his arm around his wife. "Is he someone you've known for a while, Cam?"

"He's a new guy," Dylan butted in. "He's rich and weird. Kind of a loner —"

"I didn't ask you," his father said abruptly.

"Whoa, excuse me. No normal kids allowed, right?"

Cam and Alex looked at Dylan's over-the-top outfit, sagging baggies, hugely oversized parka, fat, unlaced high-tops, two earrings in one lobe, blue-streaked blond hair, moussed at weird angles. They burst out laughing.

"Freaks." Steaming, Dylan left.

"I guess I'm not surprised this happened today," Dave mused. He kissed the top of Emily's head, then beckoned to the girls. "Come into the den." He led them through the pantry out into the front hall and opened the door to his at-home office. "There's someone you should meet. It's on his advice that we decided to be extra cautious about who you see for a while."

A thin man in a black homburg hat was sitting in the armchair next to Dave's desk. His back was to the door.

"Lordship," Dave said. Slowly, the client turned. His hat brim was low over his forehead; still, there was something luminously pale about his face. He removed his hat with bony white hands.

Cam sucked in her breath and clutched Alex's hand.

His hair was ice-white, kinky, thinning. In places his pale pink scalp showed through, shiny as silk.

"You . . . you're the bleacher-creature," Cam said.

"Cam," Dave scolded.

Alex breathed, "Doc."

He smiled at her, nodded.

"CYBI, he's the old policeman," Cam decided.

"CYBI?" The old man looked at Dave.

"Can You Believe It," Alex translated. Then agreed with Cam. "That witchy gray-eyed cop's partner, right?"

"Don't call her witchy," the old man said in his peculiar raspy voice. He chuckled dryly. "She prefers 'Goddess.' As for me, I don't mind 'Doc.' Certainly I prefer it to 'bleacher-creature.'"

"Doc? You're really real? I was beginning to think I dreamed you." Alex was amazed.

"I did," Cam said. "I did dream him, lots of nights. Dad, what's he doing here? Do you know him?"

Dave put an arm around Cam's shoulder and held her tight. "Baby, he's the man who arranged your adoption."

Alex paled. Well, that explained why he'd dumped her here, she thought, withdrawing her hand from Cam's.

"Then you must know my . . ." Cam was saying. "I mean, our real mom —"

"All in good time." The fragile old man held up his hand to stave off Cam's question. "Call me what you will, but my actual name is Karsh," he confessed. "Have you been approached yet?"

"Approached?" Alex asked.

"By the messenger," Dave explained. "The one sent to lure you to Thantos."

"Dad . . . Dave . . . you know about him?" Cam was shocked. "Are you . . . like us?"

"Like enough to have served and protected you these fourteen years," Karsh confided. "But no, David is not exactly like you. He is more like . . . like Sara was."

"My mother?" Alex stiffened.

"Your devoted protector," Karsh gently corrected her.

"I tried to tell you before," Cam whispered. "Sara wasn't our mother. She couldn't have children —"

Alex whirled on Cam. "How do you know? You don't know anything."

"I . . . I've been doing some research. On my computer. I was going to tell you, Als. I tried to tell you just now. But you were too busy trashing my . . . my mom. Or Emily, or whatever I'm supposed to call her." She turned

110

to her father. "Does Mom know, too — about us, about the messenger?"

"No, honey," Dave said, then he looked to Karsh for help.

"I thought it best — a protective measure," Karsh explained to Cam. "For you, for her . . ." The old man coughed. His voice, when he spoke again, was strained; it was still coarse and grating, but barely above a whisper. "There is much you must learn, my dear ones. And little I can tell you now. But I'll . . ." He grinned his thin-lipped grin. "I'll give it a shot. Stay, David. You might as well. You've proven your loyalty to Camryn — and to Alexandra."

"And it's been my pleasure," Dave said. "But old friend, Lord Karsh, why didn't you tell me there were two of them? Twins."

"You might be more comfortable sitting," Karsh suggested. And they did. Dave moved piles of paper off his old brown leather sofa and they arranged themselves on it: Dave in the center, with Cam snuggling against him, Alex on his other side, leaning on the armrest, chin in hand.

"The questions," Karsh began. "The universal questions: Who are we? Where did we come from? Where are we going?" He rubbed his hands together. "Let's start at the beginning. Your beginning, actually. Not *the* beginning. I'm far too tired to go all the way back."

They were born, he told them, two minutes apart on a most auspicious day — October thirty-first. Halloween. One of them was born listening to owls call and bats shriek, just as the full moon was setting; the other, a moment after daylight, squinting into the rising sun. And they were named for Apollo, the sun god, and his twin sister, Artemis, the hunter.

Their mother's name was Miranda.

CHAPTER TWELVE
THE BEGINNING

Miranda glanced out at the fading moon. Pale and full, it lingered in the morning sky. Already, the new day shone through the window. Its golden rays lit the tiny, perfect infants she held in her arms.

The first born, Artemis, stirred restlessly against her, while her sister, Apolla, but a few minutes old, slept deeply and contentedly.

Sitting beside them was their father, Aron. In his strong hands he held the magnificent necklaces he had fashioned for them, hammering delicate gold into sun and moon. For it had been foretold that their birth would bridge the day and night.

Miranda was already wearing the wondrous necklace her husband had made for her. Its pendant was a perfect circle composed of sun and moon. It cleverly matched the two amulets, the sacred charms he'd created for their children, which fit together into a perfect sphere.

Weary, Miranda closed her eyes and drifted off to sleep, aware of the fragile, warm weight of the newborns in her arms and of her husband's joy and wonder.

"Aron." There was a knock at the cottage door. "I need a word with you."

"Thantos?" Aron rose, smiling. "Come in, brother. Come see your nieces . . . *Uncle* Thantos," he added, chuckling.

"I am not alone," came the gruff reply. "And who is with me, you would not have in your home. Come out, then, come to us."

Aron went to the window. It had been clear a moment ago, its heavy shutters thrown open. Now the glass was webbed with dense, icy frost. He shook his head. What was this? Another of Thantos's tricks? His brother had been dabbling in strange magick lately.

Aron strained to see through the door. Impossible. And his own fault. He had used the precise materials and cast the proper spells to ensure the house's privacy. Not even his legendary senses — his impossibly sharp sight, hearing, sense of smell, taste, touch — could penetrate the walls.

He could feel the blinding pain, the fierce headache that came with pushing his powers to the limit, and still he could make out nothing but Thantos's shadowy bulk.

Miranda shivered. "Wait, wait," she called out in her sleep.

Aron, too, felt a sudden draft. He drew on his warmest cloak, woven by Miranda from the wool of their favorite lambs. Then he covered his beloved wife with the absurdly large quilt she had made for their babies. It smelled wonderfully of the flowers she'd used to dye the pieces and the magical herbs with which she'd filled each lovely panel.

Again she moved restlessly. And flailing Artemis stretched out her tiny fist to him. "I'll be back, my darlings," Aron promised, starting for the door.

Just as he reached for the handle, Apolla awoke with a cry. On impulse, Aron hurried back to them. He slipped their amulets on, kissed Miranda and each of his daughters, and, with a heavy, incomprehensible sorrow, left them.

Forever.

Some time later, Karsh entered the cottage. He used the key Lord Aron had entrusted to him. Bowed by grief,

Karsh sighed miserably as he saw the still-sleeping Miranda.

Something stirred beneath her quilt; some creature squirmed in the crook of her arm. Karsh stared, amazed, as a tiny clenched hand, no bigger than an acorn, emerged from beneath the coverlet.

Holding his breath, the old tracker tiptoed to the couch. There he saw the babies. One of them, the one who'd shaken a miniature fist at him, wriggled fretfully in her sleep; the other one was wide-awake but silent, calm, content.

Karsh hurried back to the door. "Come, young witch. Hurry. Miranda has had her babies," he called.

"I don't want to be a witch," the sullen teenager, his ward and protégée, replied. "Witches are ugly and have warts and wretched hair —"

"You read far too many mainland magazines, Ileana," Karsh gently scolded her. "Come, child, it is an inspiring sight on such an evil day."

Flinging back her long, silky hair, Ileana reluctantly entered the cottage. Her beautiful face was pale and tense from the ugliness she had just witnessed. There were angry tears in her striking gray eyes — eyes the same color as Aron's had been. And in her delicate hands she carried the handsome lamb's-wool robe Lord Aron had been wearing. It was sticky, still wet with blood.

Ileana, sixteen years old, about to turn seventeen, quietly crossed the room. Karsh realized the girl was shaking. He reached to put an arm about her but she shrugged him away. "I am perfectly fine, old warlock. I don't need comforting," she announced.

Prideful, like her abandoning father, Karsh thought. And yet he adored the child. For in addition to her arrogance, Ileana had an unquenchable curiosity that kept her humble — whether she liked it or not. There was nothing in the world of witches and warlocks or, for that matter, in all the vast mainland that she did not want to know, experience, experiment with, and improve. She was an avid and demanding pupil. And Karsh enjoyed nothing better than teaching young fledglings how to sharpen and use their skills.

Still clutching the bloody cloak, Ileana bent down to examine Artemis. The infant's weaving hands caught hold of the teenager's hair and tugged at it with awesome force. Delighted as she was surprised, Ileana cried out.

At last, Miranda awoke — startling Apolla, whose little wrist was twisted in her golden necklace.

Ileana untangled the chain. "Oh, but this one is exquisite, too," she remarked.

"My daughters." Miranda smiled sleepily. "Do they not resemble their father's illustrious family?" She noticed the robe then. Caught the scent of wool first. The wool and something else. Something overpowering and bitter. "Aron?" she exclaimed, then saw the blood.

Miranda began to thrash. She ripped her husband's cloak from Ileana's hands and buried her face in it.

Quickly, Karsh rescued the babies. He handed them to Ileana and put his arms around their grief-stricken mother. He rocked her as she screamed in horror. He held her thrashing head against his chest and crooned comfortingly to her even when, in an effort to silence her own earsplitting screams, she sank her teeth into his shoulder.

Finally, she wore herself out and grew quiet, shuddering and trembling.

Ileana took the newborn twins outside, while Karsh rinsed Aron's blood from Miranda's face and hair. "Tell me, Miranda, when did he leave and why?" the white-haired old warlock asked.

"Thantos came," she answered dully. Karsh nodded and tenderly wiped her cheeks, her closed eyes. She had stopped crying. And shivering. She had, in fact, stopped everything but rocking back and forth. "Thantos called him. Aron asked him in, but Thantos would not enter. Aron left to speak to his brother —"

Pacing just outside the door, Ileana heard. She held the babies tightly, muttering under her breath. Lord

Thantos, Aron's own brother, had murdered their father. Had left them fatherless, just as she had been left . . . Ah, but these two still had a mother. The magnificent and powerful Miranda. Who called out suddenly:

"My babies? Karsh, where are my babies?!"

Ileana returned to the couch. "Here, Lady Miranda. Here are the little ones. They're well. And I'll keep them that way — for as long as you wish. No one will hurt them, great lady. No one. Ever!"

Miranda did not look at her daughters. Instead, she studied Ileana's face, strangely, her eyes drifting unfocused over every feature as if trying but failing to memorize it. "Who are you?" she asked in the barest whisper.

"Ileana," Ileana replied. "I am Lord Karsh's ward —"

"I know you. I know your father. Please do not harm my children. Please, I beg you!"

CHAPTER THIRTEEN
FREE EDDIE

"David?" There was a gentle knock at the door. "I'm sorry to disturb you, but dinner is ready. Perhaps your client would like to join us?"

"It's Emily," David told the old man. "I'm sorry. I didn't realize how late it's gotten. Can you stay?"

"Oh, please, say yes," Cam urged him. "You can't leave now."

"She's a terrific cook," Alex promised. Cam raised an eyebrow at her. "I didn't say she was the Mother of the Year," her twin grumbled.

"My goodness," Karsh said, "it's nearly dark outside. Ileana will be furious with me. She's waiting to take me home —"

"Ileana, your partner?" Cam asked. "Is she the same one who saved us when we were little?"

Karsh nodded. "From that terrible day forward, she's been pledged to guide and protect you." He stood slowly and began gathering some old documents from Dave's desk. "You mustn't make her work so difficult." He chuckled.

"Difficult?" Cam echoed, then clapped a hand over her mouth, as Emily asked through the door, "I'm sorry. What did you say?"

"Give us a minute, Em." Dave looked at Karsh, who shook his head. "I'm afraid my client won't be joining us," he said, "but we'll be out soon."

Cam jumped up. "But you can't —" she began.

"Leave you?" Karsh shook his head. "Never — so long as I have life left. I made that promise long ago." He glanced at Dave, as if asking his permission to go on, and Dave understood and nodded. "I made that promise to your dying father —"

"And to our mother?" Cam wanted to know.

"Yes," the old warlock said sadly. "Though I was never sure that she heard me."

"Well, where is she, then?" Alex demanded. "And where has she been all these years?"

Karsh continued to sort through the documents. When he didn't answer Alex's question, Cam threw another one at him. "Will we be able to contact you when we need you? I mean, do we go through Dave, or what?"

Dave shook his head. "I have no way of reaching him," he said quietly.

"Regretfully," Karsh confirmed, "there is no way." He turned to Dave. "I've left you the birth and death certificates. And filled in, to the best of my knowledge, the other information you requested —"

"Where is she?!" Alex repeated. "And why should we believe you? Why should we believe anything you say?"

Finally, the old man looked at her. "I'm sorry, Artemis. Alexandra. Which do you prefer?"

"Alexandra," Alex said definitely.

Karsh nodded. "I know how deeply you miss Sara. I know how devoted you were to each other. Like David, Sara had excellent instincts and intuitions. Far greater than the average person. Her senses were finely honed, though nothing compared to yours and your sister's. You are both already far advanced as seers and healers. Even in infancy, it was clear that you were as extraordinary as had been predicted. At some other time and place, perhaps Sara might have developed her own skills and gone beyond being an adept. In time, she might have become a guardian. But she chose, as did David, to be a protector, to use all of her gifts to guide and guard a more skilled fledgling —"

"Fledgling. There's that dumb word again," Alex cut him off. "We're not baby birds. We're human —"

"Or are we?" Cam whispered.

"Indeed you are," Karsh assured them. "All too human. Did you imagine that witches and warlocks were a race apart? So many of limited vision and shriveled spirits have thought that way," Karsh said, surprising Cam and Alex with a note of pained bitterness.

He cleared his throat. His voice, however, never sounded clear, but grating and, more often recently, weak. "We are human beings — all of us. Even," Karsh couldn't help adding with a grin, "that inept but good-hearted son of yours, David. Dylan. The boy has possibilities."

"I hope not," Dave joked. "Two teen witches are quite enough."

"Are we witches, then?" Cam wanted to know. "Really?"

"It's what they call us nowadays," Karsh answered. "But there have been people like us through the ages. Seers, sages, shamans, sibyls. Those whom others depended upon for wisdom, healing, help. And we of the Coventry clan carry on that tradition. We have chosen, like Sara and David and thousands of others, to use our unique abilities to serve and protect those in need."

Someone began to clap — slowly and rudely. Cam

and Alex heard it, though Dave seemed not to. "For goodness' sake, Karsh, get over yourself. Say good night, good-bye. Thanks for the dinner invite. Gotta go!"

"Ileana!" Cam identified the voice.

"You go, girl." Alex laughed unexpectedly.

Karsh winked at them. "Catch ya later," he said, taking David's arm. "If you'll just see me to the door."

"BTW, girlfriends," Ileana said, her presence a gust of pine-perfumed air passing their faces. "Call me Goddess."

The next day, it all seemed like a dream to Cam. Her mother was not Emily or Sara. Her mother was a beautiful witch named Miranda.

For Alex, it was more like a nightmare. Sara was dead. Sara was not her mother. And whoever this Miranda was, she'd been willing to give her children away.

Emily pulled into the mall parking lot. "Are you sure you want to take the bus home?" she asked as the girls tumbled out of the car.

"Well, actually," Cam began.

Alex stepped in front of her and leaned in the front window. "No probs, Em. Nice of you to give us a lift, but mass trans works for us."

"Or maybe Beth's folks will give us a ride," Cam added hopefully. "We're meeting her at Banana."

"Banana Republican. Yeah, we can catch a lift with the Sharks," Alex said.

Emily looked dubious but shrugged and called, "Well, all right. Have fun, then," and drove off.

"It's Fish," Cam said irritably as they walked into Lord & Taylor, cutting through the menswear aisles.

"What's fish?" Alex played innocent, shouldering her way through cashmere jackets.

"Beth's last name. It's Beth Fish, not Beth Shark. And what's this sudden passion of yours for public transportation?"

"If you don't use it, you lose it," Alex said, following Cam up the escalator. "And since we're such public-minded citizens now — I mean, here to serve and protect our fellow beings — I'm for preserving mass transit."

"He wasn't kidding," Cam snarled, turning at the top of the escalator. "You are a witch. And pardon me for barging into your secret thoughts again, but what does Cade Richman have to do with this?"

"I'm going to meet him at the food court in fifteen minutes," Alex said, stepping off the moving staircase and brushing past Cam.

"And that would be because you're absolutely sure

he's not Thantos's messenger?" Cam called, hurrying after her twin.

"If he is —" Alex pushed open the door to the mall and held it for Cam. "Then Thantos sure knows how to lure me. Cami, the boy's got it goin' on."

"You think this is a joke, don't you?" Cam demanded.

"A girl can hope, can't she? And anyway, Apolla," Alex croaked, trying to imitate Karsh's voice, "maybe you believe that fairy tale he told us last night, but I've got serious doubts. Like, for instance, how come your old man's wheezing white-haired client never even answered Dave's first question? He never told us why we were separated. Why my moms and Dave never knew we were twins —"

"It's pretty obvious why," Cam said, rushing past the cart where crystals were sold, glancing disinterestedly at the accessories shop. "Thantos — that overgrown bearded bozo who killed our father. For whatever reason, he wants to kill us, too. Both of us. Together."

"Well, then, why didn't he? He found us before. Twice —"

"Because Karsh and Ileana showed up."

"And now, supposedly, *Uncle* Thantos has sent some messenger to get us. And we're supposed to figure out who it is and not get caught. If Ileana can be disguised as a cop or a waitress or anything she wants to be, then so can the messenger probably. I mean, it's like beware of everyone."

Cam saw Beth waiting in front of Banana Republic. "Hey, girl." She waved to her best.

"If you are a girl," Alex added, trying to make her voice all spooky. "And not some tall, kinky-haired clone from the evil side of the Coventry clan."

"Make sense much?" Beth said frostily. "Ugh, don't look now but there's a felon behind you."

Of course Alex turned. As did Cam. "Eddie Robins," she said. "I thought he was in juvie hall."

"Well, somebody must've bailed him out," Alex mused. She had a bad feeling about that.

"Don't look at him," Beth whispered. "He might come over —"

"Yo, Edgar! Whassup?" Alex called out.

The beefy boy glared at them. "You think you're real funny, don't you?" he said, stomping toward them ominously. Beth grabbed Cam's hand and took a step back.

Alex, don't mess with him, Cam silently ordered her sister. *Can't you feel it? He's in a world of pain.*

"Yo, dude. I wasn't jiving you. I really want to know what's up. Like who put up your bail — Cade?"

"Where'd you hear that?" Eddie stuck out his chin belligerently. "What's he, like, braggin' all over town?"

"Just a hunch," Alex said.

"I don't know if it was him. My old man won't tell me. He just said one of the kids I go to school with gave him the dough."

"What makes you think it was Cade, Alex?" Beth asked in a hushed tone. "I mean, didn't Eddie break into his house —"

"Didn't need to break in," Eddie announced, rubbing his shaved head. "I had the gate key. Leastways, my dad did, and I just went over there to pick up the lighter he dropped. Got it from my older brother, one that was killed in the Gulf. Patio door was open. So I went in. I was just looking around inside. I figured I could always say I thought maybe Mr. Richman found the lighter, mighta left it on a table or something —"

"And the alarm went off," Cam said.

"Oh, yeah, I forgot you was the witch sisters. What else you think you know?"

"The police found your footprints in the house," Beth blurted. Then gasped at her own audacity. "That's what I heard."

"Yeah, and that money was missing. Lots of it, right? Well, I didn't take it," Eddie snarled.

"Then who do you think robbed the place?" Beth asked bravely.

"Maybe Cade's nutso sister. I don't know. But it wasn't me — even though nobody's going to buy that!"

Cam looked at Alex, then said to Eddie, "I buy it. I don't think you did it."

"Me, too," Alex said softly. "I don't think it was you."

Eddie's threatening glare softened slightly. But his voice stayed menacing. "Oh, you don't, huh? Hey, well, I'm home free then, right? I mean, with a couple of witches on my side! Ha-ha-ha!"

"That was so weird," Beth commented as the bully scuttled away.

"Cade's nutso sister," Cam said aloud.

Alex nodded. "At first I thought the screams were from the kid's mom — the little boy, who was run over —"

"But they came from inside the car, didn't they? The laughing girl started screaming —"

Beth had been watching them, listening, trying to keep up. Finally, restless and confused, she scanned the mall. "Uh-oh, speaking of nutso. Here comes Velcro-girl."

"Oh, wow." Before they knew it, Madison was on them like white on rice. "O.M.G., I was totally just thinking about you. I cannot believe you forgot to tell me about the party! I've got, like, the best costume, too. I heard Amanda and Sukari talking about it. A sleepover, right? I just knew you forgot to invite me. Hey, like, don't be embarrassed. No big. Just give me the stats — time, place, et cetera — and I'll be there. Wait. Never mind. I'll get the details on Monday, okay?"

Cam stared after her, openmouthed. *Have you ever been able to read that girl?* she silently asked her twin.

No, and I don't like her, Alex answered. *Madison's thoughts, they're blank, dark, a jumble.*

Alex never had *heard* what Madison was thinking.

"Can we please go inside now?" Beth asked. "It's getting way too freaky-deaky out here."

"You guys go on. I'm cutting out," Alex told her. "I'll meet you later. At the food court."

"Alex, don't," Cam said. "We're not supposed to."

"Supposed to what?" Beth asked.

"Date," Cam said. *Especially not,* she added silently for Alex's benefit, *strangers.*

"We're only strangers 'cause I haven't had a chance to get to know him better. See you in fast-food heaven," she called to her sister and Beth. "At Hamburger Heaven, a million sold; only two digested."

CHAPTER FOURTEEN
A DATE WITH DESTINY

Any doubts that she had about Cade were forgotten the moment she caught sight of him.

He was leaning against the ice machine, checking out the Galleria trekkers. Lanky and cool in a black tee, clean jeans, and biker boots, his dark hair flopped casually forward onto his brow, framing those clear, blue-sky eyes.

"Hey." Alex raised her hand in greeting.

"Hey, yourself," Cade said, taking her hand and drawing her close. His lips brushed hers. And the buzz stayed in her ears and vibrated on her lips, so wonderful and loud that Alex could hardly hear what he was saying.

". . . or just wander around?" was the part she tuned in to.

"Sure," she said. "Let's wander. And talk."

"Oh, no, not that," Cade kidded. He was still holding her hand. "Anything but that."

"But we have to talk," Alex teased back. "I mean, I can't read your mind; how else will I find out what you're thinking?"

"Believe me, you wouldn't want to," he assured her. "I don't even want to."

Want to or not, it didn't matter. No matter how intensely she concentrated, Cade's mind was all crackling babble again. Alex couldn't break through the static.

"You start," he suggested. "What's on your mind?"

"Well, first thing," she said, looking around, "I'd like to check out some tunes."

"Done," Cade said, his hand on her back, warm, firm, steering her across the mall into the blue-tinted, bubble-flashing music megastore.

They walked up and down the aisles, until Alex came to the section she wanted. Cade waited while she shuffled through some CDs. "So how do you like school? Being new and all." He grinned. "See what a cool conversationalist I am?"

"Brutally chill." Alex laughed, then shrugged. "It's okay."

"Your sister's really into it. How come she knows so many kids if you guys just moved here?"

"Long, weird story. Cam's lived in Marble Bay all her life. I'm from Montana. I just got here this summer —"

"Get out." Cade was incredulous. "But you guys are identical twins. I mean, you've even got the same necklace —"

"It's not the same," Alex said, lifting the amulet so that he could see it. "Mine is a moon charm. Cam's got a sun."

Cade took the pendant from her fingers and turned it over. *Nice*, he said sincerely.

Sincerely? How did she know that?

Because he hadn't said it aloud, Alex realized. He'd thought it. She'd done it again! She'd gotten past his chaotic jabbering. Or maybe it was the necklace, the charm that had done it. The moment Cade touched it his mind had opened to her.

And now she heard him think, *Oh, no. There's Robins*.

Alex looked up. Edgar Robins was a couple of aisles away, flipping through a bunch of discounted cassettes. "Oh, there's Eddie," she said, as if she hadn't heard Cade's thoughts. "I ran into him before. He just got out of juvie. Someone from school sprung him. I don't know why anyone would do that. I mean, everyone thinks he robbed your house."

"Yeah," Cade said, rubbing the moon charm with his thumb. And then, *But he didn't. Man, I wish he had. I've got to get out of here.* "Hey, how about . . . ?"

"A slice?" Alex asked, making it easy for him. "I'd love some pizza."

Unexpectedly, Cade hugged her. "You read my mind." He laughed. As they left the store, he slung an arm over her shoulder; his hand, on the back of her neck, idly touched the necklace chain.

Alex was torn. Every move Cade made sizzled inside her. Every thought he had dumped ice water on that fire. He was thinking right now. Thinking . . . something noisy. A racing engine. Screeching tires.

She wished Cam were here. Cam could describe things that had gone unsaid.

Then, all of a sudden, Alex recognized the noise.

A car! The red convertible Cam had pictured. The speeding car that had hit the little boy.

"Do you drive?" she asked as they crossed the mall, heading for the gourmet pizza shop. "I mean, have you got your license yet?"

He seemed startled. "No," he said. "But that is so whack. I was just thinking about . . . about a car."

"Hmmm." Alex put her hand to her forehead, swami style, and pretended to be concentrating deeply. "A car. A blue . . . no, wait. A red car, am I right?"

His hand tightened on the back of her neck. "Well, yeah . . ." he said cautiously.

"Convertible?" Alex asked. But she was sickeningly sure now. "A red convertible sports car."

My sister's car, his scurrying mind was saying. *Karen's BMW. How does she know?*

"The little boy," Alex said abruptly. "What happened to him?"

Cade freaked. "Cut it out," he hollered, leaping back. "What are you, a witch or something?"

"I guess," she answered, relieved.

He didn't know she was a witch!

Warmth flooded her again, replacing the breathless chill she'd gotten when she thought Cade might be the messenger.

But the little boy . . . crushed as she was on Cade, the little boy who'd been hit by his sister's car meant more to her now.

"Is it her child? Your sister's?" she asked him.

He shook his head no.

Again Alex wished Cam were here to see what she could not. Thinking of her twin, she mindlessly toyed with her necklace — feeling, on the mottled face of the half-moon, the delicate dents Aron's hammer had left.

What had Karsh called it? An amulet, a sacred charm. The sacred charm her father had made for her. Her father.

She'd always known that Ike Fielding, with his stupid get-rich schemes, big talk, and bad debts, could not have been her real father.

And then her thoughts were interrupted by a steady, pulsing hiss. Shoes squeaking on a linoleum floor. Rubber-soled shoes. Efficient shoes. Like the ones the nurses taking care of Sara had worn. Steady beeps. A monitoring machine.

"The little boy — he's in a hospital."

Cade stared at her. Gone was the pleasure, the warmth she'd seen in his bright eyes. Fear had replaced it. Fear and then shame as he nodded yes. The boy, the child his sister's car had hit, was in the hospital.

"I . . . I've got to go. I'm sorry," Cade said, flustered, angry, ashamed. "I've got to get out of here."

Alex watched him stride away, caught a last glimpse of him as he disappeared into the crowd at the mall.

Alex. I'm waiting. Let's go, girl. Where are you?

She looked around. No one she recognized was near.

Hello. Impatient, sarcastic. *Alexandra. We're at the food court.*

No one she knew called her Alexandra. Except Madison. Ugh. The girl really was a pain.

But the summons Alex had just heard. It hadn't been spoken aloud. It had been *sent.* So it couldn't have been Madison.

Could it?

CHAPTER FIFTEEN
HEALING HERBS

"Lucky you, you just missed your biggest fan," Beth said as Alex approached their table at the food court. Cam's willowy best was munching her way through an order of french fries.

"Who, Cade?" Alex asked hopefully.

"Not exactly," Beth answered, licking ketchup off her fingertips. "Weren't you with him?"

"Madison," Cam told her. "She was waiting for you. Then all of a sudden, she split. You know how antsy she is."

"Did you, um . . . call me?" Alex asked her twin.

"Duh." Beth hiked her head at Cam. "The digital diva forgot her cell phone. Quick e-mail News at Eleven."

I did, Cam answered her sister. *You were late. I was worried.* Taking in Alex's flushed face, she forgot herself and asked aloud, "What happened? What's wrong?"

Alex couldn't answer with Beth staring at her. "Nothing." She reached over to Beth's plate and snagged a handful of fries. To Cam, privately she announced, *We have* so *got to talk!*

While Alex sucked down the filched fries like strands of spaghetti, Cam felt a headache coming on. It was the one she always got when the visions started. Closing her eyes, she saw, in a series of lightning flashes, Cade Richman's horrified face, the speeding red convertible, an oxygen tent set up in a hospital room, and Madison Knudnick grinning impishly. *Whoa, girl.* Cam's eyes flew open. *You are throwing way too much at me at once.*

"What do you mean?" Alex asked.

"Cam's right. You don't look all that well," Beth answered. Pushing back from the table, she gathered up the shopping bags mobbed at her feet. "We'd better boogie. My mother's probably waiting for us —"

Cam started to get up. Alex stopped her. "Gee, I told Mom we'd be taking the bus," Alex said.

"Mom?" Cam was flummoxed. "Excuse me?"

Hello. I was trying to sound normal, her sister informed her.

139

How are you spelling that, D-O-R-K?

Actually, yes, Alex sniped back.

Beth shrugged. "Suit yourself, Armani. E' you later."

They were barely on the bus when Alex began to unload on Cam. "Okay, first of all, you were right, right, right. Eddie was telling the truth. About not robbing Cade's house, anyway. Don't ask me how, but Cade knows that Eddie didn't do it —"

"You read him!" Cam squealed, delighted.

"It wasn't easy. Until he started fooling with my necklace and then, open sesame noodles, I knew what he was thinking. And one of the things was that red convertible you saw. It's a —"

"BMW," Cam said. "Of course."

"It's his sister's car. Nelly Nutso . . . only her name's Karen. And Cami, the little boy. She did hit him, or whoever was driving that car did. And he's not dead!"

"Is he the one who's in the oxygen tent, in the hospital room?"

"He's definitely in a hospital. But I don't know which one or where. I don't even know where the accident happened. Do you?"

Cam shook her head. "Dark road, that's all I saw. Dark road, the red blur, top down, headlights, a kid running —"

"And I heard the laughing," Alex added. "Coming from the car. And then the screams and the . . . the sound, the terrible sound, when they hit . . . the boy, I guess. But why would a little kid be running across a dark road? Was he alone? You didn't see his mom or anyone with him? I mean, maybe if you try —"

"Oh, no," Cam said forcefully. "Give me a break. I don't want to go back there now. My head's just starting to feel better."

"Well, what are we going to do? I mean, I didn't *see* any of it. The hospital room, Cami. Can you zone in on, you know, like a chart or something? Those plastic bracelets they wear? If we just had the kid's name, then we could check out hospitals until we find him."

"And when we do? I know what you're thinking — that we could save him, cure him, fix his bones or brain or whatever is wrong with him. But this is a person, a child, a real human being, Alex. He's not —"

"I know, I know." They had fixed things before. Things, not people. Cam using her phenomenal sun power and Alex the amazing hearing that told her what was happening in the dark. Together, they'd bent iron to their will. But could they mend a broken boy the same way?

Alex turned her back, looked out the bus window — as if that would hide her doubts from Cam.

They said nothing for a time. Then, when they were almost at their stop, she felt a hand on her shoulder. Its touch sent an icy shiver through her.

"Karsh did say we were born healers —"

Alex twisted around and stared at her look-alike. Cam's eyes were unfocused, barely open. She was squinting in pain. "And that we're supposed to help people," she said, her voice shaking.

"You did it." Alex wrapped her arms around her shivering sister. "You went back. You found him."

"Not really." Cam shook her head. "I found his name. N. Tung, I think. I don't know which hospital. But the room . . . The beds are all in a circle with partitions but no doors. The nursing station is in the middle of the room. I saw 'ICU' and a girl with a cart. . . . She was wearing this pink apron and talking to a nurse."

"A cart?" Alex asked.

"You know, with juice, magazines —"

"Stuff that candy stripers give out?"

"The apron!" Cam remembered. "That's what 'Manda wore last year when she volunteered at Mount Bay Medical!"

"And ICU stands for Intensive Care Unit. He must be in bad shape," Alex said dully, remembering that her mother — no, Sara, she reminded herself, feeling tears welling, blurring her sight. Sara had died in a long, crowded ward down the hall from the brightly lit, carefully monitored Intensive Care Unit.

Alex realized that she was still hugging Cam. Feeling dumb, she let go, but her sister clung to her.

"Als," Cam whispered. "What are we supposed to do? I don't know anything about healing —"

"He said herbs," Alex recalled. Closing her eyes, she rested her chin on Cam's head, on a cushion of clean, thick auburn hair. *Get to know your herbs and flowers,* Doc had told her back in Crow Creek — Doc, whose real name was Karsh. *Study your crystals and stones. You've already got a flair for incantation —*

But which herbs and flowers, crystals and stones, which incantations or spells would they need to help a very sick little boy?

"The only herbs I know anything about are herbal bath foams and shower gels," Cam confessed. The bus lurched to a stop. "O.M.G., this is us." She jumped up, banging Alex's chin. Then, grabbing her hand and hauling her to her feet, Cam dragged her sister off the bus.

Ten minutes later they were racing up the stairs to their room, when Emily called, "Alex, that boy phoned. Cade Richman. He's been calling every ten minutes for the last half hour. He left his number."

"I don't want to talk to him," Alex replied, not even stopping.

"Cade called and you're not interested?" Cam asked when they were in their room.

"I'm totally ticked at him," Alex decided. "He knows Eddie didn't steal money from his house. I heard him thinking that Eddie didn't do it. So why didn't he tell the police that, instead of getting his dad to pay Eddie's bail? I mean, that's pretty lame."

"Cade's dad is the one who bailed Eddie out?"

"'Looks that way. I mean, Cade wouldn't have the cash. However bustable Eddie is, if he didn't rob Cade's place, he doesn't deserve to go to jail for it —"

"I've got it," Cam shouted, digging in her knapsack for her cell phone. "'Manda."

"'Manda what?" Alex asked, annoyed at the quick convo switch.

"She's, like, into all this alterna-stuff — especially herbs, right?"

"But she's not a witch," Alex reminded her.

"Do you have a better idea? Got Karsh's digits? Or Ileana's? I'd love to call them but, duh, I don't think they're listed."

The cellular rang the minute Cam laid hands on it. "Amanda?" she asked.

"Whoops, another rank mojo failure." Bree laughed. "But you get partial points. She's here. We're at Sukari's. Scoop time, Cam-era. Someone from school broke Eddie out of juvie!"

"Saw him. Talked to him. Galleria. Today," Cam announced. "Put 'Manda on, please."

Alex rolled her eyes and plopped down on her bed. Then she jumped back up again. The crystal Karsh had shown her after Sara's funeral . . . when he'd said that Alex would make an excellent healer . . . where was it? Had she seen it in her duffel bag?

While Cam grilled Amanda, Alex searched the beat-up canvas carrier Karsh had packed for her. And found the faceted pink gemstone.

She drew it out, feeling it grow warm in her hand. It reminded her of that terrible day, the funeral, the wrenching loss of Sara. . . . Tenderly, Alex rubbed the heated crystal with her thumb. And thought suddenly of violets — Sara's flower.

Violets, mint, chamomile, she heard. Karsh's raspy voice whispered the names of the medicinal plants. *Rosemary for contentment. Sage, of course. It gets its name from the Latin word for healing. Thyme, to inspire courage.*

The voice changed abruptly. *Oh, for goodness'*

sake! The edgy, crooning complaint could only be Ileana's. *Get your sister off the phone. Now. She knows where the herbs grow.*

"What about the boy?" Alex asked, revolving slowly, looking around the room, checking the ceiling. "Where is he?"

Do I look like OnStar? Ileana sounded indignant. *Use a little ingenuity. Let your fingers do the walking. Try the telephone book.*

"Excuse me. What are you doing?" Cam's hand was over the receiver end of her mobile. She was staring at Alex, alarmed.

"Hang up," Alex told her. "Like now!" She dived for the Yellow Pages stashed under Cam's night table and started riffling through the book, looking for hospitals.

Cam's gray eyes blazed rebelliously. But she said, "Thanks, 'Manda. I think I've got it all. BBGF," and clicked off her cellular.

"BBGF?" Alex didn't look up from the phone book.

"Bye-Bye, Girl Friend," Cam said coldly. "Amanda recommends chamomile, mint, and thyme."

Alex hid her astonishment. "Three out of six. Not bad," she said evenly. "Did she tell you where to get them?"

"I don't need Amanda to tell me," Cam declared. "I know where to go."

* * *

Mariner's Park was at its most peaceful in late afternoon. Though it was still light out, by five o'clock the families who used the playground and sailboat pond had gone home — as had the checkers and chess players and the bystanders who commented on their every move. The elderly had evacuated their benches and the teens who gathered after dinner had not yet assembled.

Alex and Cam walked along the pebbled path in silence for a time. They had checked the three hospitals listed in the phone book. One of them, Mount Bay Medical — the hospital where Amanda had been a candy striper for a summer — had a patient named N. Tung. Nguyen Thanh Tung, a little Vietnamese boy. "We call him Nelson," the ICU nurse had told them. "He doesn't know that, of course. Cutest little fella you ever saw, but he's still in a coma. I'm going to miss him."

Cam had gulped, thinking the nurse meant Nguyen was going to die — until the woman added, "They're moving him to a private room as soon as one becomes available."

"Here it is," Cam said, breaking the silence. They turned onto a dirt trail that wound through trees and brambles up to the park's highest point, a hidden, gently sloping field that offered an awesome view of the harbor below. At the center of that secluded meadow was a thick, weathered elm tree.

In that hidden place, under that ancient tree, Cam had often found solitude and serenity. The sweet perfume of thyme, which carpeted the meadow, pleased her senses, as did the tufts of wild mint and chamomile and violets nestled among stones and pungent, prickly sprigs of rosemary. . . . The little field was rampant with soothing herbs and wildflowers, which, up until today, Cam had simply thought of as pleasant plants.

Whether listening to her Discman or writing in her journal or just staring up at the clouds or out at the water, it was one of the few places in Marble Bay where Cam was perfectly content alone. She'd shared her private haven with only one other person — Alex.

They trudged out into the open now to gather the herbs they needed.

What they found was an intruder.

Cam couldn't believe her eyes. But even before she zoned in on the trespasser, she recognized the face, half-hidden behind stringy brown hair, and the energetic, pint-sized body. The little gnome was sitting in the grass, leaning back against a tree — Cam's tree, the big old elm she loved.

Madison Knudnick seemed almost as stunned to see them as they were to see her. For the first time, she wasn't lively, jumping around, shrieking in that nasal whine of hers. She was, in fact, brooding. *Send a man to do a child's job*, Alex heard her say gloomily, before Madison spotted them and whatever else the girl was thinking got lost in static again.

Madison scrambled to her feet. "Wow, is this, like, too weird for words? I didn't know anybody else knew about this place. But, well, of course you two would. Duh." She smacked her forehead. "Like how could you not, right? Still, I've gotta say you, like, totally freaked me out, stepping out of the woods like that."

Cam believed her. Madison looked radically stressed. Honestly surprised. And, Cam realized, "honestly anything" was not a phrase she'd ordinarily use to describe the manic mouse-ette.

But Alex wasn't as convinced. "How did you know we were going to be here?" she demanded.

"Hello," Madison sang. "Anyone home? I just told you, Alexandra, you guys scared me to pieces. I had no idea you'd be here —"

"And by, 'of course we'd know about this place,' you meant?" Alex probed.

"Well, everyone knows this is a . . . a . . . you know, like, historic area —"

"I've lived in Marble Bay all my life," Cam informed the wheedling girl, "and no one ever mentioned that to me."

"Oooo, my mistake, I guess. Totally you'd know better than me. I must have gotten it all confused with, like, some other place."

"Some other place that's famous for what?" Cam pressed.

"O.M.G., I am so late!" Madison looked at the giant watch that looped loosely around her little wrist and started backing away. "Supper time. Gotta run. See you guys at school."

They stared at her, a hundred questions racing through their minds, as she skittered away, disappearing like a scrabbling animal through the brambles.

CHAPTER SIXTEEN
THE DECISION

Karsh stopped to smell the wild mint. It grew in knee-high clusters behind Ileana's cottage. He leaned for support against the trellis he'd built for her more than a dozen years ago, when she'd become guardian of the twins. The youngest guardian in Coventry's history. At his insistence.

Rhianna, Grivveniss, Karkum, Shiva, and old Cho, who'd since passed on, had thought he was mad to suggest such a thing. Perhaps he was, Karsh allowed. Mad with grief over what had happened to Aron. And to Miranda.

He had assured the Unity Council, of which he was then a senior member — was it only two years ago that he had retired from the ruling body? Ah, well. He had promised them that Ileana would rise to the occasion, though she was young, only a year older than the twins were about to become, Karsh realized.

Soon, very soon — next week, in fact — they would celebrate their fifteenth birthdays. Proof that though he might have been addled with sorrow when he appointed Ileana their guardian, he had not been wrong. They had survived, hadn't they? Survived and thrived. And would soon prepare for their initiation into the clan.

Karsh sighed and righted himself. "Ileana?" he called. "Are you in the garden?"

"Karsh, Karsh, I did it! I imitated your voice perfectly," she answered happily. "Not as perfectly as if I'd transmutated, but they thought it was you. At least Artemis did — until my impatience gave me away. She's the one I spoke to. Listen."

Through the bayberry hedge, he saw her sandaled feet resting on the table she'd had shipped from the mainland. Ileana had ordered the wrought-iron "garden set" from a Web site called Hollywood Chic — and when Karsh had balked at the price, she'd lectured him on stylishness and elegance. This was, of course, shortly after her trip to Los Angeles. Where it was not just "stylishness" she'd fallen for, but Brice Stanley, the handsome warlock who'd become a movie star.

Ileana set down her laptop, frightening Boris, who

was on the table, lazing in the sun. He bounded away as she hopped up from her stylish wrought-iron chair and hurried to meet Karsh. "Violets, mint, chamomile," Ileana chanted in a strange, choked voice. "Sage, named for the Latin word for healing. Thyme, to inspire courage."

"Is that what I sound like?" Karsh asked, amused.

"Exactly," Ileana assured him.

"Well, I'm impressed —"

"With my impersonation?"

"That you remember your lessons on medicinal herbs. But you might have been more helpful to them —"

"Why? You've always believed in letting *me* learn through doing. They may be of noble blood but even princesses can profit from practice. For instance, transmutation —"

Weary, Karsh cut her off. "Truly, Ileana, I'm very impressed with your knowledge of —"

"Medicinal herbs, healing plants! Pooh!" Her gray eyes sparked angrily. "I only helped them to perfect my morphing, to show you that I am ready. I want to transmutate like a tracker. Like you! I don't care what she thinks. I want to do it."

Karsh hobbled through the archway in the hedge. And, unexpectedly, Ileana took his arm and helped him to one of her mail-order chairs. "By she, I assume you mean Lady Rhianna?" he said, easing himself onto the cold metal.

Ileana glanced around her wooded yard then up at the sky to be sure no surprises would sail into view. "Lady Potato," she whispered, though no one was in sight, "can get baked for all I care. With melted cheese and chives! The girls — *my* girls," she emphasized, "are in trouble. Thantos has sent someone to snare them. Or maybe he himself has transmutated! It's such an easy thing for a tracker to do. Maybe Thantos didn't send someone else. Maybe he has shape-shifted into the messenger."

Karsh was staring at Ileana's computer. There it was, emblazoned above the screen, the 3Brothers logo. Thantos's company had manufactured the machine and, probably, most of the software it took to run it. So rich, and yet so greedy, Karsh thought.

Ileana marched over and abruptly shut the laptop screen. "Okay, so I'm e-mailing Brice. Big deal. We've been . . . corresponding. Is that a crime?"

"Do you know who donated this computer — and all the others — to the island?" Karsh asked.

"Don't change the subject. I was saying that Thantos might even have morphed himself into the messenger! And face it, Karsh, you're far too old to take him on. But I could —"

"He would not be a messenger," Karsh said. "Lord Thantos is a busy man. A warlock used to 'delegating responsibility.' Getting others to do his bidding . . . his despicable dirty work."

Ileana stared curiously at Karsh. There was acid in his gravelly voice, a biting anger she'd rarely heard. What did he mean, what long-ago time was he thinking of, remembering? What terrible dirty work had Thantos assigned to someone else?

"Lord Karsh," Ileana said tenderly. He looked so weak, so fragile. Before she knew what she was doing, she had knelt before him. The thought of her beautiful silk cloak crumpled in the grass around her, her pale gown driven into the dirt by her own knees, disturbed her. But she brushed away such selfishness — for the first time, she realized.

"What makes you so . . . sad, Lord Karsh?" Ileana asked with a gentle affection that touched the old man's heart.

"You are right," he answered, "I am far too old." Taking her hand, he drew her to her feet, then he himself stood slowly. "I am no match for Lord Thantos. Let us hope I can still charm Lady Rhianna. She will be furious —"

"You're going to teach me to transmutate!" Ileana exclaimed.

"Yes, my brave dragon slayer." Karsh rubbed his dry, papery palms together. "Gather the proper crystals and herbs? Let us begin . . ."

CHAPTER SEVENTEEN
THE MUMMY

"I hope it won't be bad karma," Amanda said, handing her candy-striper uniform to Cam in the hall outside their lockers. "Look." The inside of the pink apron was stamped, PROPERTY OF MBM. "Mount Bay Medical. I totally forgot to turn it in."

"So that's why the cops came to school last week," Sukari teased. "Dag! And I thought it was to bust Eddie Robins."

"If this stunt goes wrong, they may show up again to arrest Cam," Beth grumbled, totally forgetting that she'd been sworn to secrecy.

"Stunt? What stunt?" Bree's satellite dish picked up Beth's blooper.

Alex stepped in front of Beth, who was wringing her hands and going, "Stunt? Who said stunt? Did I say stunt?"

"Thanks a bunch, Beth." Alex put on a disgusted face. "Now everyone knows what Cam's wearing for Halloween."

Bree's eyes narrowed suspiciously. "Never," she said finally. "Like Cam would really come to her own birthday party in an apron! So not."

"Alex was going to be my patient," Cam insisted, working hard at keeping a straight face. "Weren't you, Als?"

Alex took a CVS bag out of her locker and began pulling out endless rolls of gauze bandage. "Well, I guess that blows that idea," she said. "Gee, sis, we'll have to come up with something better."

"That shouldn't be too hard," Kristen remarked. "A hospital volunteer and a patient? How ill. I mean, whoever thought that one up must be seriously damaged."

It was Wednesday. Emily's book club night. Dave's chance to catch up on office work at home. Dylan was scheduled to meet his posse at the local skate park after school. And Cam and Alex were supposed to be having dinner at Beth's.

So it was all set. Mrs. Fish would pick them up at

school and drop them at Mount Bay Medical, where, Beth had explained to her mother, they'd be participating in a Halloween party for the patients.

"But what are you going as?" Beth's mom asked her daughter as the trio scrambled into the backseat of the Fish family SUV — Cam in her hospital volunteer apron, Alex with her head and arm bandaged like a mummy, and Beth in the same DKNY outfit, Kate Spade bag, and Skechers sports clogs she'd worn to school.

"A rich kid," Alex mumbled through her bandage-muffled mouth.

"Oh, you mean like Cade?" Beth shot back.

Cam elbowed Beth. "Cut it. You know she's not speaking to him."

"I know that, but not why." Beth sounded offended. "Or why I'm supposed to let you guys know if I spot him at the hospital."

They'd told Beth how crucial she was to their mission. And for Cam, she was.

"What if this is a trap?" Cam had asked Alex two nights ago. "What if Thantos's messenger just wants to get us alone, like at a hospital where we don't really know anyone?"

"We'll deal with it," Alex promised. "All we need is a scout, a lookout —"

"Who'll be looking out for what?"

"You know. Possible, uh . . . messengers," Alex had said uncertainly.

After an hour of squabbling, they'd settled on three suspects: Cade (Cam's vote); Mr. Shnorer (Alex's candidate); and Madison (who'd won two thumbs-up).

As for their lookout, Dylan was in enough trouble, they decided. He couldn't afford to get mixed up in another risky scheme.

So it was — unanimously — Beth.

Who, right now, in the back of the SUV, was all bent out of shape because they had asked her to help them though they didn't explain why.

"After all, Camryn," she was complaining, "I'm just your humble servant, no longer your trusted confidante." Leaning forward, she told her mother, "I'm going as their humble servant, Mom. My costume's at the hospital."

"Confidante? After that blabbermouth move you pulled?" Alex snapped.

"How many times do I have to apologize?" Beth asked. "It was a mistake, okay? My bad. Big whoop."

"Bethie, you are my confidante and best bud in the world," Cam assured her. "And I'm, like, totally grateful for your help."

"Me, too," Alex said. "The grateful part, anyway. I

just don't feel like talking about Cade right now. He . . . he's not who I thought he was."

"I hope he's not who I think he is," Cam put in. "Beth, have you seen Madison at all this week? I have English with her and she never showed up —"

"No, but so weird. I forgot to tell you. She sent me an e-mail message. She's sick or something —"

"What's so weird about that?" Cam asked.

"I never gave her my e-mail address. Anyway, she said she's, like, totally psyched about your party and she wanted to know what everyone was going to wear. You know, like, who was going as what. She said she'd be there no matter how sick she was."

"Speaking of missing English," Alex said, "Shnorer skipped out today, too. Amanda said she saw him going into Mrs. Hammond's office this morning, looking grossly bummed. And we had a sub for class —"

Beth's mother pulled into the circular drive in front of the hospital and dropped the girls off. "Call about fifteen minutes before you're ready to come home, all right? Kiss, kiss, Elisabeth. Have fun, girls."

They waited and waved until the car was out of sight. Then Cam took a deep breath and said, "Okay, Alex and I will hit the emergency room and try to snag a wheelchair. Beth, you find out exactly where the boy is. Which floor. His name's New-yon —" She pronounced it as the telephone receptionist had. "But the nurse said they call him Nelson . . . Nelson Tung."

The emergency room entrance was at the back of the hospital. While Beth hurried inside the front door to the patient information desk, Alex, leaning on Cam's arm as planned, hobbled around the side of the building.

"Have I got everything?" Cam nervously patted the bulging pockets of Amanda's apron. "The herbs. Your crystal. The incantation we made up. Do I have that or do you? Never mind, I know the words. I think. Let's see, I brought a couple of aroma candles, just in case. You know, one for stress, the other for wisdom. I hope I brought the wisdom candle. It's the same color as the romance one. Oh, and the violets —"

"I hope you brought a paper bag to breathe into," Alex murmured. "'Cause you are having a first-class meltdown. Hyperventilating up a storm. It's going to look pretty funny, with these bandages and all, if I wind up having to wheel you in."

They came to a loading dock at which two ambulances were parked. On the platform, a wheelchair stood at the ready. Cam scrambled up the steps to get it, while Alex waited below, crouching behind one of the emergency vehicles.

"Hey!" A driver barreled out of the other ambulance, flicking away a smoldering cigarette with two fingers. He had a spare stashed behind his ear. "That's hospital property. Hands off, honey." Smoke snaked from his lips as he shouted at Cam.

Alex hollered back, "And that poster says, 'No Smoking. Oxygen in Use,'" she advised him, pointing to the large sign on the loading dock.

The startled driver stared at her. "What is this, *Night of the Living Dead*?" he snarled. "Halloween's a couple of days away, girlie."

"Not for you, it isn't," Cam said suddenly, her eyes riveted on the cigarette behind his ear.

"I said, leave that chair alone. Do I have to call security? You're playing with fire here, honey."

"Oh, gosh, Cam. He guessed." Alex laughed.

"Don't get smart with me."

"She can't help it," Cam told him, her burning eyes beginning to tear. "She's my twin."

"Don't make excuses, Cami. This guy's IQ is below room temperature."

"That does it," EMS man growled.

"Hi, I'm Alex. I'll be your server today," Alex said as Cam's glare connected and a curl of smoke drifted from the driver's spare cigarette. "How would you like your ear? Well done, medium, or rare?"

Beth was waiting at the elevator bank. "Fifth floor,

room five eleven," she told them. "I still don't get it, though. You had some premonition about this little boy, this Nelson whatever — that he needed your help?"

"How do we look?" Alex switched the subject.

"Like a hospital volunteer helping a deranged mummy."

"Forget it," Alex said. "We'll meet you back down here."

"I've got my cellular," Cam confirmed. "Don't forget to speed-dial me if you see —"

"I know, I know." Beth sighed, resigned. "Madison, Shnorer, or Cade."

CHAPTER EIGHTEEN
THREE SUSPECTS

He was already there.

They didn't notice him right away. The first thing they saw when Cam wheeled Alex into room five eleven were enough flowers and potted plants to fill a garden.

A short, stout woman, the circles under her eyes almost the same color as her graying black hair, sat in the midst of this bright jungle. She sat alongside a hospital bed, holding the limp hand of a little boy and talking to him in a language Cam and Alex didn't understand.

Tubes and wires flowed from the child's arms, chest, and bandaged head to monitoring machines behind him; machines partially hidden by a vase of bright orange birds-of-paradise set among huge tropical ferns.

"Are you Mrs. Tung?" Cam asked gently.

That was when Alex realized he was in the room. Cade.

He was standing behind a ficus tree, its pot wrapped in tinsel paper and decorated with a big red ribbon. He was leaning against the window, his head pressed against the glass.

When he heard Cam's voice, Cade turned. Alex dropped her head, pretending to be dozing, hoping he wouldn't guess who she was, that no blue hair was sticking out of her bandages.

"Alex?" he said at once. But he was looking at Cam.

Cam jumped. "What are you doing here?"

"You first," he said. "You're not her. You're her sister, right? The twin."

"Camryn," Cam confessed. "I . . . I work here." She smoothed down her pink apron as if offering proof.

"What are you, some kind of volunteer?"

The child's mother was looking back and forth, from Cam to Cade, trying to keep up with the conversation. It was clear she knew very little English.

"I'm a candy striper," Cam said smoothly. "I'm taking this patient to her room." She glanced at Alex, whose bandaged head was collapsed onto her chest. "I must've gotten the room numbers mixed up."

"No biggie," Cade said. Then, turning to Mrs. Tung,

he spoke very slowly and gestured with his hands. "I'm going to see the doctor, okay? Find out how Nguyen is doing. This girl — from school. She's a friend." He nodded at Cam and walked out, without so much as a glance at Alex.

"It's not him. He's not the messenger," Alex said the minute he was gone.

Cam hesitated. She'd gotten nothing but honest vibes off the boy. Still, what was he doing here?

Guilt, Alex answered. *It was his sister's car. For all we know, his sister was driving it.*

"What if *he* was?" Cam whispered. "What if Cade was the driver?"

"He doesn't have his license," Alex said lamely. She didn't want to think about it. One look at him had set her back days. She could feel her anger and distrust melting away, her heart growing tender, warm. But Cam was right. What was he doing here?

Cam smiled and nodded at Mrs. Tung. "Whoops, what's our plan B?" she said softly to Alex. "I didn't think about his mom, or anybody else, being in the room. We'd better take off, I guess."

"Stay, stay!" a raspy voice invited them. "I'll just be a moment. I'm going to talk with Mrs. Tung."

"Doc! I mean, Karsh!" Cam's arm felt all tingly from where his starched lab coat had brushed against her.

"Right you are," he answered. "And what are you supposed to be?" he asked Alex, with a very un-Doc-like touch of sarcasm. "Let's hope no one scrapes a knee in this town, there's probably not a shred of bandage left."

Turning his back on her, he addressed the boy's mother. "Madame Tung," he called her, and bowed. And began speaking in an Asian dialect, which the grateful woman quickly responded to. The next thing they knew, Doc had led her out of the room.

Alex jumped out of her wheelchair and peeled off the bandages. Cam had closed the door and begun emptying her pockets, spreading out at the foot of the bed the little pot of crushed herbs, the bouquet of violets, Alex's pink crystal, the paper on which they'd written their spell — and two aroma candles, one of which was labeled ROMANCE.

How doable is this? Alex wondered, looking for the first time at the little boy in the bed. He was very pale. She could see his blue veins under his sallow skin. His lips were dry, parched, swollen. For a moment, she closed her eyes. *Oh, please, please help us*, she thought.

Help us to help you, Cam added, staring at the child's yellowing bruises.

Guide us —

"Okay, let's do it, shall we?" Doc was back in the room, rubbing his hands together. His fingers — was

Alex imagining it? — seemed just a smidge thicker than Doc's normally bone-thin joints. "That wasn't the spell, was it," he said, sighing. "I've heard better from no-talent novices."

They'd just been warming up, Cam told Karsh defensively. Alex picked up the crystal, which began to heat at once. Cam held the violets, which she'd intended to wave under the boy's nostrils — but now, seeing that he had a breathing tube in his nose, she wasn't certain what she'd do with the little flowers. Cam and Alex held each other's hands and stared uncertainly at the incantation they'd written out.

Karsh broke in, instructing them to hold the boy's hands, as well. "The healing energy will come from you. Flow through you. I'll take care of the accessories." He held out his hands — which looked far more delicate than Alex remembered — and they deposited their magick preparations in them.

"See him truly," Karsh instructed. "Listen to the blood pulsing through him. Feel his body's needs. Read his mind's will. Offer him your strength in exchange for his weakness."

But they were already doing that. The moment they laid hands on the boy, sights and sounds assailed them. The jagged break that ran along his skull. The slosh of bruised marrow in two shattered ribs. Sizzling red germs massing like an army of fire ants in his crushed ankle.

The battered boy couldn't speak with his mouth, but his entire self was whispering to them. And his brain, inside the broken skull, his brain was whole and healthy and desperate.

"Not bad." Karsh laughed. "I'd leave out that big-headed 'my' before 'moon magick' and 'curing sun.'" He was reading over their incantation. "Otherwise, you've written quite a nice little spell. Go on, then, recite it."

Alex began: *"Universe of love and health . . ."*

"I think I need the herbs now." Cam held out a hand for them and Karsh, grinning proudly, poured the green flakes into her palm. *"Use these gifts of nature's wealth, to heal this child who wronged no one,"* Cam said, sprinkling the fragrant powder over the sheet covering Nguyen.

"With my moon . . ." Alex began.

Karsh shook his head at her.

"Uh, with . . . moon magick," she corrected herself, *"and curing sun."*

"Stand back!" Karsh cackled, raising his hands.

Suddenly, the twins were drawn together with such speed and force that they banged heads over poor Nguyen. "Our necklaces!" Cam shouted.

"They're locked," Alex realized, feeling the violent pull of the gold chain on the back of her neck, and heat rising off the joined charms.

"Help!" Cam squealed.

"Do not forget your mission," Karsh warned. "Focus on the child!"

And, in that uncomfortable position, faces mashed together across the bed, they tried.

"Universe of love and health,
Use these gifts of nature's wealth,
To heal this child who wronged no one
With moon magick and curing sun."

The monitoring machines began to blink crazily. Nguyen stirred. "I'll go find his mother," Karsh said, rushing out of the room faster than they'd ever seen his old legs carry him.

"Wait!" Alex hollered, but he was gone.

"Oh, this is fun," Cam grumbled, trying to tug apart their locked amulets. "Now we're conjoined twins."

A tiny voice mumbled something.

Alex and Cam looked down. Nguyen's mouth was moving. And then his eyes flew open. He was as startled to see them tented above him as they were to hear his sudden surprised giggle.

Thank you, oh, thank you! Cam was crying.

"Cut it out," Alex whispered, but her eyes were also

wet. And a moment later, she, too, was chanting, *Thank you, oh, thank you*, because their sun and moon charms had flown apart, tossing them backward into separate banks of flowers.

A nurse, who'd seen the remarkable change in Nguyen on her computer at the nursing station, ran into the room just as Cam and Alex left.

Hurrying toward the elevators, they passed the visitors' lounge. Cade was sitting there alone, his head in his hands. Instinctively, Alex took a step toward him, then stopped.

"Go on," Cam urged. "I'm going to speed-dial Beth and tell her I'm on my way down. But Alex, until we find out who the messenger is, please, please be careful."

Alex hugged her sister. "Totally," she promised, then went into the lounge. "Hey," she said, and Cade looked up.

"Hey, yourself. Was that you in the mummy suit?"

Alex laughed. "I was pretty surprised to see you there."

He stared at her for a moment, then looked out the window. "My sister did it," he said. "She was driving home, with her roommate. Nguyen ran out into the road and she couldn't stop in time. She hit him. Hit and run —"

"I sort of knew that," Alex admitted, sitting down beside him.

"Well, the police don't. And neither does my father. He'd have her arrested or locked up in some loony bin if he found out. Karen's been getting into trouble since she was a kid, since our mom died. She never really got over it —"

Alex sighed. "Trust me, I understand."

Cade turned back to her. "I sort of knew you would," he said, taking her hand. "My dad, he put way too much on her. On Karen. She was only thirteen and he thought she ought to pitch in, take Mom's place. She was supposed to be like his little hostess and housekeeper, and a substitute mom to me. Plus he started traveling a lot about that time."

"I'm sorry. But still . . ." Alex squeezed his hand. "I mean, what's that got to do with the robberies and Eddie?"

"I took the money," Cade said. "I stole it — from the house, from my dad. He leaves a lot lying around —"

"But why?" Alex asked. "Does it have anything to do with the other girl in the car? Was she driving?"

"Jennifer? No, she is . . . I mean, she *was* Karen's college roommate. Jennifer Shepherd. They were freshmen together at Newton. But it was Karen. I wish it wasn't. Karen was driving."

Alex nodded, closed her eyes.

She seemed to be listening to something that Cade couldn't hear.

After a moment, as if she were talking in her sleep, she said, "But Jennifer, the roommate, she had something to do with it, right? With the robberies."

She heard an argument. Two girls quarreling — over the fallen boy's body, she guessed.

We've got to get him to a hospital!

Leave him, Karen. Let's go.

No, we can't. Jennifer, help me. Do you have your phone? Call 911. Hurry.

You want to tell the police you were doing seventy?

Was I?

Come on, Karen. You're hysterical. I'll take you home. Your headlight's smashed. There's probably blood on the car. If your dad's there, we'll say that you hit a deer or something —

No. We can't leave him. He's hurt. He's just a kid and he's hurt bad.

Karen, get real! I'll come back. I'll take care of him, okay? I'll take care of everything. Let's go!

"Jennifer," Alex said, opening her eyes with major effort. She felt dizzy now. There was a ringing in her ears. "Jennifer Shepherd. She's . . . blackmailing your sister."

Cade nodded yes. "I bring her money every month.

Cash. No checks. She's back in school now. Prescott Newton Junior College, just outside Boston. Karen dropped out. She can't do anything. She's a basket case."

Jennifer Shepherd at Prescott Newton. Alex filed it away.

"Karen told me everything," Cade continued. "I didn't know what to do. So I came to the hospital. And I saw him. I recognized him. He's Vietnamese. His mom cooks for the people next door to us. Nguyen used to visit her on weekends. I let them use our pool. I guess he went swimming and was running back across the road, to the Bannister house, where his mom works. It's just a dirt road through the woods. You hardly ever see a car there —"

"And you've been giving her money, too — Nguyen's mother?" Alex said.

"For the hospital bills. Their insurance doesn't cover much."

Don't think of Sara, Alex warned herself. Stay focused.

"And for flowers, sometimes." Cade shrugged. "Mrs. Tung likes flowers. And we take turns talking to Nu, his mom and me and Karen —"

"Your sister's been here?"

"Yeah. A lot. And, believe it or not, she's as bummed

about Eddie taking the blame as you are. And as I am," he confessed. "It's over. Karen and I are going to the police. I was just hoping Nu would improve. It'd make it easier. Karen's in such rotten shape. The only time she seems okay is when she's holding his hand and talking to him. Sometimes you can almost believe he hears her, and he's, like, trying real hard to get better."

"You never know." Alex smiled at him. "That might make all the difference."

Cam stepped off the elevator in the lobby. Beth was waiting. Eagerly.

"They were here!" Leaping from her chair, she breathlessly repeated what she'd told Cam on the phone. "Shnorer and Madison. They both showed! I was going to call you a second before you called. Shnorer probably did his pen-throwing trick again, only whoever he tossed it at this time must've hurled it back. I don't know, but he came in clutching his paw and yowling about blood poisoning — even though there wasn't a scratch on him!"

"Where is he now?" Cam pressed.

Beth guessed he'd gone to the emergency room. She hadn't kept track because, like a minute later, she explained, Madison had appeared. The girl seemed not the least bit fazed to find Beth in the lobby. "I just came for my final checkup," Madison had said smoothly. "My fever's way down and I think — party-wise — I'm good to go!"

"How freaky-deaky is that?" Beth demanded. "I mean, two out of three of them showing up!"

"Try three out of three," Cam told her. "Cade's upstairs."

"Not even!" Beth was flabbergasted. "So, what are we going to do? Should I call my mom to pick us up or are we staying?"

The elevator dinged. They glanced at it as the doors opened and Alex charged out. "Beth, think your mom could drive us to Boston?" she asked, dashing toward them.

"Absolutely not," Beth replied. "Anyway, what *new* do-good mission would I tell her we're going on?"

Alex said, grinning wickedly, "This one's strictly a do-bad!"

CHAPTER NINETEEN
TIME TO PREPARE

Ileana gave up. That's what she told Karsh. "I give up. I just give up. I don't know how you ever kept track of them."

She had come knocking on his door. Naturally, she hadn't waited for him to answer it. She'd dashed in, cape swirling, thick makeup blotchy, the nappy white wig sitting crooked on her head.

What a fright she looked. Karsh's breath caught at the sight of her. Ileana, pale as death and dreadfully wrinkled. Was that how he looked?

She must have been in a great hurry to have returned to the island in this condition. A good sign, Karsh decided, as the shock of seeing her passed. Never before had Ileana's vanity permitted her to be in public looking less than perfectly beautiful.

"Come in, come in," he said, although she had already rushed past him and was pacing his book-lined parlor.

"First let me say that I was marvelous. Flawless. Camryn and Alexandra accepted me as you without question. I was fully, brilliantly disguised. And my voice was perfect!"

Oh, no, Karsh thought. Ileana was walking past the large gilt-framed mirror over his fireplace. He hoped she would not be disturbed by her image.

Another first, he marveled. She passed the mirror without a glance.

"After instructing the twins in proper healing procedure, I left them in the hospital room," she explained, "and I woke the nurse at the monitoring station so that she'd notice the boy was coming to. Then I spoke with his poor mother and explained that something wonderful had happened, that she should return to her son's room. There I was — thanks to your stubbornness, knowing only the basics of voice transmutation — wearing a wig, pounds of greasy makeup, and that depressingly shabby lab coat —"

Ileana strode back and forth across the oriental carpet — which had flown long ago, but being older than

Karsh, was now grounded by age. "And then I felt the chill," she confided, whirling suddenly, "and I knew that Thantos's underling was near, somewhere in the hospital! AIEEEE!!!"

The hair-raising cry made Karsh clutch his heart.

"Look at me! Look!"

As Karsh had feared, his ward had caught sight of herself in the mirror.

"How could you let me wander around like this?" Ileana demanded, scrubbing her face with the hem of her cape.

Her scream had startled him so, he'd nearly lost sight of what was important. "You met the messenger?" he asked urgently.

"I felt its presence. And of course I raced to find the children. I ran back to the room where I'd left them. But they were gone. Gone! Can you imagine how terrified I was? With Thantos's evil minion roaming the hospital. And I . . . suffering, sick with worry, wondering, even as I searched, whether the messenger might already have found them. Confound it, Karsh!" She hurled the wig across the room. "Am I to be cursed with your pasty skin and penciled wrinkles the rest of my days?"

"Less, if you calm down. What did it look like?" Karsh insisted. "Did you recognize the person? Old, young, tall, stout, male, female? Was it even human? Tell me!"

"I've been thinking," Ileana responded with cruel casualness. She threw herself into Karsh's favorite easy chair and rested her legs on his beloved old hassock.

She kicked off his black velvet slippers, which had hung large and lopsided from her toes. "What if Thantos, who is, of course, a master of transmutation, really did decide to go after the girls himself? I know you said he would not. But . . . couldn't he have shape-shifted, turned himself into another creature, morphed into the messenger? The chill I felt was amazingly strong — as was the stench of evil that came with it."

"It's possible. But as I told you, Thantos is quite used to putting others to work, using them to carry out his orders," Karsh said, agitated, angry.

There it was again, Ileana noted, the strange change in Karsh's attitude when she suggested that Thantos might be the messenger.

Ileana sat up abruptly. "Great and venerable tracker, what are you saying?" she asked sweetly. "What terrible secret have you kept? What is it that you know and I may not?"

Now it was Karsh's turn to pace. "Only what I said," he answered roughly. "Lord Thantos has made a habit of shirking responsibility. Of letting others handle tasks he considers beneath him. A very bad habit. Tell me, did you find the twins, Ileana?"

"I did. When I last saw them, they were in the hospital lobby, trying to coax their freckle-faced friend into getting her mother to drive them to Boston."

"For what purpose?" Karsh wanted to know.

"I didn't stay to find out. I tried to track the messenger. But I lost the scent in the emergency room. There, so many other smells overpowered it. Alcohol, iodine, disinfectants —"

"Why would they want to go to Boston?" Karsh wondered aloud.

"Shopping, I suppose. Marble Bay is no Beverly Hills. Except compared to Coventry."

Karsh was thoughtful. At last, he smiled. "You seem nearly recovered, Ileana. More yourself again. It's time, I think —"

"Time?" Ileana looked at him curiously.

"Time to prepare —"

"Karsh . . . Lord Karsh . . . Do you mean it?"

He nodded yes. "You've earned another lesson in transmutating. One you may be called upon to practice soon."

CHAPTER TWENTY
HIT AND RUN

At lunchtime on Friday in the high-school cafeteria, Cam whispered to Alex, "We can't cut last period. And I'm not taking a bus to Boston. Not the day before my Halloween bash."

"But it's a classic op. I already told Emily we had some last-minute party shopping to do after school. I just didn't say where or how long it might take. Or . . ." Alex grinned at Beth. "How we'd get there."

"What's that supposed to be, your winning smile or something?" the willowy girl grumbled. "Does the phrase 'forget about it' work for you? How about, 'no way'?"

"Right," Cam said. "And how about, 'no bus —'"

"Spoiled much? Anyway, it's not like skipping *class*. It's just a safety-rules assembly. Marble Bay's fire chief is going to tell us not to play with matches, okay?"

"Hello?" Bree's fork, dangling a nibble of lettuce, stopped just short of her mouth. "What are Mary Kate and Ashley plotting today?"

"They're going to *college*," Beth sneered, doing a great imitation of Brianna, Cam thought, taken aback.

"Baaaap! You're out of the game show, Fish," Alex announced, "for not knowing the meaning of *secret*."

Surprised at her own outburst, Beth looked apologetically at Cam. "I'm sorry," she said softly. Aware again of Bree's gaze, she went back to her aloof act. "But, like, I thought you wanted me to go with you. I didn't realize it was just a chauffeur you needed and that my mom was the stooge of choice."

Bree cackled appreciatively. "You go, Fish."

"O.M.G., Go Fish. It's a card game!" Kristen giggled.

Amanda shook her red head sadly. "You guys, you're so negative. I mean, we're all working for a peaceful planet, aren't we? Just ignore them," she advised Alex.

"Yeah," Sukari said, "everyone else does."

"Well, here comes someone who won't." Bree began to wave frantically. "Jason, oh, Jason! Camryn's got a favor to ask you."

"Bree, that's not funny," Beth scolded as Jason Weissman, the shy senior who everyone knew was crushed on Cam, came toward them.

"Well, Cam and her clown — whoops, I mean clone — need a ride, don't they?" Brianna protested. "And who has a license and a pizza delivery truck?"

"Déjà vu," Alex whispered to her twin. Jason had bailed them out before, when they'd needed a lift to help rescue the pop star. "Hey, Jason." Alex smiled big at the tall, dark, and studly boy.

"Hey," Jason responded, his face totally turned to Cam.

"Want to cut assembly and drive us to Newton?" Alex asked him, just to see if he was still conscious. A handsome hottie, Jason became a major Moe around her sister.

"Sure," he answered, still not looking at Alex.

"You don't have to," Cam said, shooting Alex a dirty look.

"No problem," Jason said.

It was as simple as that. They didn't even have to ride in the PITS van. Jason's own wheels, an ancient but lovingly restored Volvo, was parked in the student lot. And Alex didn't mind stretching out in the backseat. In fact, it was an excellent place to jot down notes for a powerful hex.

"What rhymes with Shepherd?" she called out to Cam, who was chatting up their driver.

"Shepherd?"

"Jennifer Shepherd. She's the girl we're going to see."

"Oh." Cam scrunched up her face thoughtfully.

"How about peppered?" Jason asked.

"Major snaps!" Alex congratulated the boy.

Prescott Newton Junior College was a girls' school a few miles outside of Boston. Its ivy-covered brick buildings were decorated with smirking gargoyles sticking out their tongues.

Alex reciprocated the gesture as the Volvo stopped before the arched entrance to the school. Jason said he'd wait for them at the visitors' parking lot, and they promised to meet him there as soon as possible.

"The question of the day," Cam said as they headed for the administration building, "is what do we do if and when we find her?"

Alex passed her the pad on which she'd written the spell.

Oh, cheater of your roommate
You caused so many pain
Now accept your fate
And end your blackmail game.
Free Karen Richman,
Oh, Jennifer Shepherd,

Or you'll be assaulted . . .
And peppered.

Cam groaned. "Assaulted and peppered?"

"I thought it was cute," Alex said defensively, grabbing back her pad. "You know, like salt and pepper; *assault* and peppered."

A loud, shrill laugh distracted her. Alex turned toward the group of girls gathered on a nearby bench. One of them, a pretty brunette, was hysterically amused.

"I know that laugh. Is that her? Does she look like the girl in the BMW?"

Cam glanced at the same crew. "The one in the red sweater? Yes! That's exactly how she looked."

Alex trotted across the lawn to the bench, dragging Camryn with her.

"But we have no herbs, no crystals, no stones," Cam protested. "Just that . . . um, *thing* you wrote."

"It's not a thing. It's an incantation," Alex pointed out irritably. "And anyway, we also have your mojo and my mean streak."

Conversation on the bench grew hushed as Cam and Alex approached. The red-sweater girl looked them up and down, then burst out laughing again. "Just in time for Halloween," she erupted. "It's Cinderella — before and after."

"And what are you going as — a felon?" Cam questioned her.

"A . . . what?" one of the other girls said. "Duh, I totally don't get it."

"What my sister means," Alex explained with a smile, "is that your friend Jennifer —"

"You are Jennifer Shepherd?" Cam asked her.

"The shepherd and her sheep." Alex took in the staring crowd. "You were in the car with Karen, weren't you? That would make you an accessory —"

"Oh, no, no," Cam insisted. "An accessory is something that brightens up a boring outfit."

The brunette stood up slowly. She seemed to be uncoiling rather than getting up. She was tall, way taller than Beth, Cam realized as the girl glared down at them.

"I don't know who you are or who sent you," she said, reaching into her pocket and pulling out a handful of bills. "But why don't you take a dollar or two, and go play trick-or-treat on someone else."

Jennifer was a regular riot. At least her crowd thought so. Giggling and elbowing one another, they laughed at Cam and Alex.

But Alex's attention was on the crumpled bills in Jennifer's hand. She wondered if the careless heap of cash was money Cade had given the girl.

Cam was on the same page. *Dirty money*, Alex heard her thinking.

Blood money, Alex silently amended. Which gave her a monster idea!

Golden, Cam agreed, tuning into the plan. *But can we do it?*

"Worth a try," Alex said aloud, handing her the incantation again.

Cam skimmed the work. "Got it," she said. "Now what?"

Alex took her hand. "Let's say it. I just hope our amulets don't act up again. My neck's still sore."

"Oh, cheater of your roommate," Cam began, *"who caused so many pain."*

Jennifer's friends were giggling harder than ever now.

"Accept your fate, and end your blackmail game," Alex recited, to loud guffaws of laughter.

"Free Karen Richman, oh, Jennifer Shepherd," Cam intoned, grateful that the final line was Alex's.

"Karen?" someone asked. "Wasn't she your roommate, Jen? The one who had the breakdown?"

"I really liked her," another girl offered. "I couldn't believe it when I heard she dropped out."

"Or you'll be assaulted," Alex vowed, *"and peppered!"*

That did it. Although Jennifer had gone pale, the girls around her had totally lost it. Breaking up, they were bent over double with unrestrained hysteria.

But Alex was focused on the currency Jennifer was holding . . . which had begun to bleed.

"Hey, no fair. Wait for me," Cam grumbled, taking Alex's hand and shifting her own gaze to the bundle of bills.

"Ugh! That is so icky," one of the college girl's clever friends shrieked. They had all stopped laughing.

"Jennifer, your money. It's, like, all bloody!" another scholar chimed in.

Dirty money, Cam was thinking. *Filthy. Putrid. Polluted.*

"And it stinks!"

"O.M.G., it smells just like poop!"

The lot of them were prancing around, holding their noses and looking dangerously queasy. Then someone gasped. "Maggots!"

The bills in Jennifer's hands were suddenly seething with slimy white creatures that looked like writhing rice.

"Drop it! Let go!" her friends were hollering, even as they backed away from her, sickened.

Violently wagging her hand, Jennifer was trying desperately to do just that. But while the white worms that had begun to mass at her wrist flew every which

189

way and the putrid stench also took wing, the bleeding money stayed stuck to her.

"Help me," she pleaded to Cam and Alex, who were the only ones still near her.

"No probs," Alex said. "Just come with us —"

"To the Marble Bay police station," Cam added.

"Anything!" the trembling, spooked-out girl promised. "Just get this money away from me!"

CHAPTER TWENTY-ONE
HALLOWEEN

Eddie was off the hook. Cade's dad refused to press charges against his son. Karen was slated for therapy. Jennifer was charged with extortion. And Nguyen was on the mend.

There was nothing left to do but celebrate!

Except that in the car, on the way home from the police station, a strange feeling crept over Cam and Alex. More like a nonfeeling, really. It wasn't loneliness, exactly, or depression, or even disappointment. It was just this windy emptiness, as if all that they'd accomplished meant nothing. For starters, they still hadn't figured out who the messenger was. But that wasn't it.

Dave, at the wheel, sensed that something was wrong. Even Emily picked up on it, too.

Only Dylan, sitting between his sisters in the backseat, was too psyched to notice that neither Cam nor Alex was answering his fast and furious questions. "How'd you find out that Cade took the money? Where'd that girl who smelled like toxic waste come from? Why was the Vietnamese lady crying?"

"What is it?" Emily finally asked when they got home. She pushed back a length of Cam's hair that had fallen over her beautiful gray eyes. "Sweetie, it's your birthday —"

"Big whoop," Cam said. Sighing, she followed Alex upstairs.

That was just it, she thought. It was her birthday. Hers and Alex's. Their first one together. And all they really knew about their birth was that it was also the day of their real father's death. He'd been murdered by his own brother. Their uncle. Who, supposedly, wanted to kill them, too. Talk about dysfunctional families!

What they didn't know was way more important. Like what had happened to their mother.

The answering machine in their room was blinking. There were five messages they didn't bother listening to — and more on e-mail that would also have to wait.

"Happy birthday!" Beth phoned a little while later. Alex was stretched out on her bed, staring at the ceiling. Across the room, Cam sat at the desk, with her feet up. Though she was nearest the phone, she had let the answering machine pick up. "So what are you going as tonight? Call me!"

They didn't say anything for a while after Beth hung up. Then, without looking at her sister, Alex asked, "So what did Doris Bass say? Tell me again."

Cam toyed with her necklace, zipping the charm lazily back and forth on its chain. "Well, to tell you she loved you and that lots of people have been asking for you and sending regards —"

"About my mom," Alex cut in. "About Sara."

"Mrs. Bass went to school with her," Cam replied. "She said Sara couldn't have kids. And she knew your, uh . . . dad, Dwight."

"Ike," Alex said coldly. "That's what they called him."

"She didn't think much of him," Cam said uncomfortably.

"Neither did I," Alex assured her, still staring at the ceiling. "Losing him is like the one bright spot in this whole mess."

Cam glanced over at the bed, then turned away. "It

isn't about them, is it?" she said softly. "It's about her, right?"

"Miranda. What kind of funky name is that?" Alex asked.

"You think she's dead?"

"Might as well be for all the good she's done us."

"I don't think so." Cam decided.

"Thantos," Alex agreed.

"He said he could take us to her."

"Maybe he meant to her grave." Alex had tried to sound laid-back, but it came out sounding angry.

"I know. I thought of that," Cam said. "How messed up would that be?"

"Hey, I lost one mom about a month ago," Alex answered. "What's one more? I can handle it."

"I can't." Cam let her feet fall, pushed out of the chair, crossed the room, and flounced down on Alex's bed. "You know, if he caught us or whatever — Thantos. I mean, if I ever saw him again, I'd go with him. I'd tell him, like, 'Okay, take me to my mother.'"

Alex kept staring at the ceiling. Finally, Cam asked, "Would you?"

"If you went I'd have to, wouldn't I? Emily would never let me stay here alone. And I definitely couldn't pass for you —"

A moment later, Alex sat up. "What *are* you wearing tonight?"

"Ugh. I was going to wear my soccer uniform," Cam confessed. "I thought that would get a laugh, the way I blew the big game last season. It just doesn't seem all that funny now. What about you?"

"I was going as myself. That always gets a laugh," Alex retorted.

"No, seriously."

"Seriously. Only now I've got this killer idea. It'll totally blow their minds."

By six o'clock the Barnes' garage had been turned into a curtained, jack-o'-lantern-lit, spiderweb-draped cave. Dylan and his crew were in charge of decorating and haunting it.

Beth was the first to arrive at the birthday blowout. A shrieking maniac in a ketchup-soaked sheet swinging down from a garage beam greeted her. To get into the party props, she was forced to shut her eyes and put her hand in a dish of worms, which felt a lot like soggy spaghetti. Dylan himself offered her the eyeballs — peeled grapes floating in lukewarm water.

Alex seemed strangely hyped to see Cam's best, who was done up as a wiry-haired Peter Pan. "Bethie!"

she shouted over the blaring CD player as the willowy girl entered the house.

"Am I early?" Beth asked suspiciously. Cam's Montana sib hadn't gotten into costume yet, she'd noticed. Unless that mess of pin curls on top of her head and the multiple jangly earrings were supposed to be it.

"I know how ticked you are with me," Alex said, taking the startled girl's arm. "I mean, my moving in here and, like, getting so much attention. But, in case you ever doubted it, Cam still considers you her very best friend in the world."

"And you'd know that how?"

"Well, uh . . . because she confides in me," Alex answered.

"Duh, give me news, not history." Beth pulled away and deposited her sleeping bag in a corner at the bottom of the stairs. "I mean, it's kind of hard not to notice that she confides in you. Have you noticed that she *doesn't* confide in me anymore?"

"Oh, Bethie, that's not fair," Alex said, running her charm back and forth on its chain.

"You see!" Beth pointed to the necklace. "Like she'd really ever let *me* wear her precious sun."

"I am so going to hurl!" It was Bree, decked out in the gown her father's girlfriend, a soap starlet, had worn to last year's People's Choice Awards. "Was that eyeball thing not totally gross? Whose idea was it, yours?" she asked, handing Alex her sleeping bag.

"Is that what they do in Montana instead of bobbing for apples?" Kristen, done up as Lara Croft, the digital action heroine of *Tomb Raider*, teased.

"No way." Cam came down the stairs. "They bob for roadkill."

"Puke-ola. Where's your costume?" Kristen asked.

"Did you cut your hair?" Bree wanted to know. "I love the shaggy look. So retro."

"Blame it on my volumizer," Cam said, fluffing her 'do. "So, where are the rest of the recyclables? Whoops, my bad. I meant the Six Pack, of course."

Bree and Kristen exchanged surprised looks, then burst out laughing. "Quick, call *ET*," Brianna snorted. "Julia Roberts just got all snarky in public."

A deep-throated chuckle announced Sukari's arrival. "You sayin' Julia's pullin' a J. Lo?" She tossed her bedroll onto the pile in the corner. "*Buenos días*, my peeps!" she greeted her buds. She was wearing a Mexican serape and sandals — but her bleached buzz cut was hidden under a red, green, and black knit cap from which frizzy Rasta dreads dangled.

"Well, if it isn't our straight-A honor student, getting down with her bad self!" Kristen high-fived Sukari. "What are you supposed to be, a vision of ethnic diversity?"

"You've heard of Salt 'n' Pepa? I'm their Latin cousin, Adobo. That's salt, pepper, and garlic powder." Sukari checked out Kris's *Tomb Raider* outfit. "Grouchy Tiger!" she declared.

"You mean, Crouching Tiger," Bree said, hugging Suki.

"No, she didn't." Beth laughed.

"Where's 'Manda?" Alex asked. "I thought she was coming with you."

Surprised at Alex's interest, Sukari answered, "She beeped me ten minutes ago saying she was feeling really sick —"

There was a scream, then a thud and a groan from the garage. Everyone turned toward the surge of sounds.

"Whew, that haunted-house scene was majorly scary." Madison entered in a pink frenzy, two soaring bunny ears poking through her lifeless hair. "Dylan's, like, sooo creative. And that guy who swung down from the beam . . . you know, the one wearing that totally barf-inducing bedsheet with all the red gunk on it? His rope snapped!"

"Oh, no! That's terrible," Beth said.

"No, no. Don't worry. I'm okay," Madison assured her. She spun around, showing off her rabbit costume, which had feet attached like the Dr. Denton pajamas Cam had worn as a baby. "Like it? Oooo, wait!" Madison reached into a pocket in her fluffy pink suit and turned her back to everyone. When she faced them again, she was wearing bunny teeth — two long, white, bucked teeth overhanging her bottom lip.

Cam broke up, as did Sukari, Beth, and Kristen. But Alex, without cracking a smile, just stared at the bizarre little rabbit. And Bree, whose mouth had flopped open at the sight of Madison, finally managed to say, "Excuse me. What planet did you say you're from?"

Dylan ran in then. "That was really rotten," he said to the tiny girl. "He could have broken his back."

Madison grinned her grotesque bunny grin. "Totally," she hissed at Cam's brother. "But he didn't, did he?"

"What's going on here?" Cam asked, turning to Dyl for an answer. But before he could respond, a redheaded witch carrying an orange cat swept into the party. "Are we having fun yet?"

"Amanda!" Alex screeched. "I thought you weren't coming."

Everyone turned to Alex, who seemed way over-elated to see their bud. Everyone but Amanda herself, who whispered to Dylan, "It's okay. I fixed your friend. Just keep him off that rope for a while."

Dylan stared bug-eyed at the witch in the peaked black hat. "Wow, you're really good at that 'whole' stuff —"

"Holistic," Amanda corrected him. "Works like a charm. Now run along."

Cam overheard the exchange. "Er . . . 'Manda?" she asked, peering at the girl, whose pale eyes didn't look blue tonight. They appeared almost gray. Black-rimmed and gray.

Seeing Cam's surprise, Amanda blinked deliberately. When her eyes opened again, they were blue.

"I . . . I must have been mistaken," Cam said uncertainly.

"What's with the orange cat? Where's Willis?" Sukari asked her best. "Willis is 'Manda's fiendish black cat," she explained to Alex, who said unexpectedly, "I know."

"Oh, really?" Kristen commented doubtfully.

"Cam knows all about Willis," Amanda said.

"You're right. Cam does." Sukari gestured at the bobby-pinned, overly earringed girl. "But that's Alex," she pointed out.

"Hello? Did someone say honor student?" Amanda's red curls bobbed like springs as she shook her head in disbelief. "Don't you get it? That's her costume. Their costumes. Cam came as Alex and Alex is supposed to be Cam."

"Not," Cam insisted. "Don't let that outfit go to your head, 'Manda. You're not really a witch."

"Actually," Amanda said, "I like to think of myself as a —"

"Goddess?" Sukari laughed.

Amanda spun to stare at her. "Totally. How did you know?"

"Oh, like you haven't checked out a gazillion books on the subject lately?" Sukari counted them off on her fingers. "*The Goddess Within, A Goddess Workbook, How to Reach Your Goddess Potential, The Goddess Diet* —"

"Excellent. Go, me!" Amanda cheered as Madison inspected the twins, her shocked gaze shifting from one to the other.

"You switched places," she accused, then added with her bizarre, bucktoothed grin, "Of course. I knew that."

The cat in Amanda's arms hunched its back and hissed at the girl in the fuzzy pink costume.

Madison cringed. "Oooo, I'm, like, deathly allergic to cats," she reported, jumping back. A chill wind followed in her wake.

"Is anyone cold in here besides me?" Amanda stroked the cat's ruffled orange fur. "For goodness' sake, what is that yucky smell?" She waved her hand, fanning the air between herself and Madison. "Ugh," she burst out. "You stink."

"Tactful much?" Bree was shocked at Amanda.

"Is that what they teach you in goddess school?" Kristen asked.

"Oh, wow. I can't help it if this bunny suit is older than Mick Jagger. Not everyone can afford a brand-new costume." Madison was indignant. And then she was crying.

Giving Amanda a how-could-you glare, Sukari rushed to the blubbering girl. "Gosh, it does feel cold here now," she said, wrapping a comforting arm around Madison. "There's, like, this bad draft . . . and . . . and . . ." Her nostrils twitching distastefully, Sukari slowly backed away.

"I need a tissue," Madison whined, staring tearfully at Alex — who was actually Cam.

"Sure. I'll get you one." On her way to the den, Cam whispered to the cat-carrying witch, "That was rancid, 'Manda. What was up with that?"

"Gosh, Cami. I'm sorry," the redhead said.

Alex took Cam's arm. "I'll go with you," she quickly offered. "I smelled it, too," she said, closing the den door behind them and flipping the lock.

"Smelled what?"

"This totally nauseating odor. It's, like, seeping out of Madison."

"Oh, Als. She explained what it was. It's that tacky rabbit suit."

"Not unless she bought it at Really Old Navy and they dragged it out of some swamp."

An icy breeze swept under the door. In her cashmere Cam costume, Alex shuddered. "And those goose bumps on your arms?" she asked her twin. "Where do you think they're coming from?"

It dawned on Cam slowly. She'd pulled three tissues out of the box for Madison before she turned to face Alex. "You're saying Madison is the messenger?"

"Still want to visit Mom?" Alex asked sarcastically. All of a sudden, her teeth were rattling with cold.

Cam sat down on the leather sofa, hugging herself. "I can't believe it. It's too bizarre."

"I second that emotion. So . . ." Alex waited. "Did you mean what you said before? That you'd go with Thantos if you had the chance?"

CHAPTER TWENTY-TWO
THE HORROR

The whish-swish of Madison's perky shuffle could be heard through the closed den door. Alex put a finger to her lips, warning Cam to be quiet — as the small girl's tiny feet, encased in the smelly rabbit suit, moved toward them.

Then, with a stench of ripe cheese, she was in the den.

Cam checked the door, which was still locked.

Alex couldn't take her eyes from Madison. She looked so strange. A pink bunny with two long teeth sticking out, looking longer, she thought, than they had a few minutes ago. But was that possible?

Yes, Cam said silently. *Definitely. Those teeth are longer and shinier and sharper —*

"Cam. Alex. How ultra-cool!" Madison squealed enthusiastically. "I totally wanted to talk to you alone."

Alex flopped down beside her twin and took Cam's hand. It was very cold. "About what?" she asked, her throat growing thick at the overpowering odor.

"About . . . your uncle!" Madison grinned. "The mighty Lord Thantos. I'm going to take you to him."

"Oh, really?" The girl, the messenger, whatever she was, was short, thin, and frail, Cam was thinking. Even if her teeth were looking dangerously sharp and had begun to separate. There was a definite space between them.

She couldn't take us anywhere, Alex agreed. *Unless we wanted to go. Do we?*

"And he," Madison continued gleefully, "the powerful, great, and revered . . ." Her two fake bunny teeth were now nearly an inch apart. "Lord Than-thos," she lisped, "can thake you to your mother."

I want to see her, Alex. Don't you?

Someday. The smell was too much. And the cold. *But not now,* Alex decided. *Not like this.*

Cam stood up, wanting desperately to hold her nose. "I'm sorry, Madison, but we're taking a pass."

Madison tilted her head quizzically. "You're what?"

Alex pushed off the sofa. "Not interested," she said, just barely keeping herself from gagging. "Not going. Thanks for the offer."

Were they imagining it or was Madison's face actually looking more ratlike? And those funny teeth, which had become sharper and moved apart — they looked like fangs now.

Cam took a step back. "Well, it's our party," she said weakly. "Guess we ought to get back to it."

The rat face turned scaly suddenly. And it was developing a massive case of zits. Red bulges burst through the rough skin. "Wow," Cam said, "that's a frantic allergy. If I'd known about it, I'd have definitely asked Amanda not to bring her cat —"

"Amandath cad? What nonthenth is thith?"

There was nothing comical about Madison's lisp. Her voice had gotten deeper and angrier. The crusty bumps on her face were rapidly turning to boils. As they grew bigger so did she.

With a loud rip, Madison's feet exploded through the bottom of her pink costume. They were also covered with boils, oozing a gooey white liquid that trickled between her toes, which were now — Alex noticed, clapping her hand to her mouth — armored with yellow nails, hooked, thick and dangerously sharp.

Automatically, Cam took hold of her sun charm.

"Really, Mad," she said in a quivering voice, "they'll be bringing out the birthday cake soon —"

"It's all chocolate," Alex added idiotically.

A great crash followed. One that stunned the twins and left them numb.

Cam shook her head, trying to regain her senses. When she could see again, Madison was gone. A gigantic beast stood in her stead. A monster with fangs and talons and bubbling lizard skin scaling every inch of its flesh.

Seeing Cam's fright, the creature laughed. The putrid odor of its breath brought Alex to her knees. And stung Cam's eyes until she was almost blind. She could scarcely make out the foul beast ripping off the last pieces of pink cloth that clung to it.

"Cam, get down. Kneel next to me," Alex commanded, grasping her half-moon necklace. The moment her sister hit her knees, Alex pushed her charm against the one Cam was still holding. The halves joined with a jolt that set the room vibrating.

"Oh, wondrous night of full moonlight," Alex began, trying to adjust to the discomfort of being fastened, necklace to necklace, to her twin again.

"Um . . . that gave us life —" Painfully, Cam opened her eyes but could see only light and shadows. *"That gave us life and took it, too —"*

"Took the parents we never knew," Alex whis-

pered, trying to stretch her gold chain just a little. *"From what was once lost and tragic —"*

"Give us now their strength and magick!" Cam blurted, surprised and pleased with herself. "Now what?"

"We need a line that rhymes with moonlight," Alex decided.

"Bright, night, fight, kite, right . . . That's it. *That we may use their might for right.*"

"Tremendous. You are so the rhymester," Alex congratulated Cam.

"I thought *you* made that up," Cam replied, squinting.

"Oh, get over yourselves," a whispery voice demanded.

"Amanda?" Cam tried to place it.

"Ileana," Alex guessed.

"Clever little T'Witches." Their guardian witch grinned.

"You?" the monster bellowed. "What are you doing here?"

Cam and Alex shuddered and ducked again.

"I might ask you the same thing, Fredo," they heard Ileana say, in Amanda's soft tones. "Except that I already know the answer."

"Smart aleck," the thing she'd called Fredo boomed.

"Whew. You are disgustingly ripe. And far too large."

"Don't get in my way, Ileana," he warned.

Cam saw an orange blur leap from Amanda's black-robed shoulder onto the monster's back. Fredo let loose an earsplitting shriek as the cat landed. "Boris! No!" His deep voice broke pitifully. "That's not fair, Ileana," he simpered. "You know how allergic I am!"

"Pity," Ileana replied, without a shred of it. "Return to your master, dog. And give him this message. Get up!" she ordered Cam and Alex. "Hold the necklaces and recite your spell."

The twins did as they were told.

Oh, wondrous night of full moonlight
That gave us life and took it, too —
Took the parents we never knew . . .

As they pronounced the spell, Fredo began to shrink. And to change form. The beast was turning back into human form — but it was not Madison emerging from the loose lizard skin. "Tell Thantos," Ileana growled at the shape-shifting thing, "that his prey have the strength and magic of their parents. And will use their power only for good. Not to enrich their greedy uncle. Not to serve their father's assassin. But to do what we were all born to do, except for your accursed family, to protect and help the innocent creatures of our world."

The creature had become a man. "You have the nerve to lecture me about these pushy brats who I've known since their unlucky birth!" he thundered. The man was beady-eyed and had a helmet of greasy black hair plastered back from his wide forehead. Wispy goat's whiskers straggled from his pointy chin. He was shorter than Ileana, and seemed exhausted from the effort of so many quick changes.

Cam and Alex were staring at him, slack-jawed.

"Don't stop," Ileana growled at them, "finish the incantation!"

Waking, as if from a spell themselves, they quickly went on:

From what was once lost and tragic,
Give us now their strength and magick
That we may use their might for right.

At the last line of the incantation, Cam's and Alex's necklaces unlocked.

They were gratefully rubbing their necks when there was a knock at the door. "Girls? Are you all right?" Emily's gentle voice asked. "I think everyone's here now. And the cake's arrived."

"We'll be out in a minute," Alex called.

"Thanks . . . um, Mom," Cam added.

They looked at Ileana in her black witch costume. She was holding Fredo — at arm's length — by the scruff of his skinny neck. The worn-out goat man glared at Cam and Alex. "Oooo, you'll be sorry," he simpered, sounding as whiny as Madison. "It's not over yet."

"If I had a ribbon —" Ileana laughed. "I'd present this sorry present to you all wrapped up. Unfortunately, I can't stay for the cake. I've got to return this smelly prize to the island. Go on, mischievous T'Witches, celebrate your birthday. Next year, you'll be sixteen. And we'll celebrate together — on Coventry Island."

"Can you see again?" Alex asked, taking Cam's hand and pushing open the door.

"Sort of," Cam said as they walked out into the hallway, which was strangely dark.

"HAPPY BIRTHDAY!" voices sang from every shadowy corner.

And then there was candlelight. Lots of it.

Thirty-one candles on a gigantic chocolate cake — fifteen for Cam, fifteen for Alex, and one to grow on — illuminated Dave's proud face, and Emily's, and Dylan and his posse, and Cam's best friends, and Cade Richman and his sister, Karen, and little Nguyen in his mother's arms, and Jason from PITS, and — could it be true? — Eddie Robins, his shaved head reflecting the dancing candlelight, his single earring twinkling, his moon face wearing a smile no one had ever seen before.

CHAPTER TWENTY-THREE
THE SACRED TREE

An old man dressed all in black climbed the hill in Mariner's Park. Halfway to the tree, Cam's tree, he stopped to mop his pale forehead and catch his breath.

"And you call me stubborn," a voice above him mocked. "I could have gotten you up this bump of grass in no time."

"It is my custom to walk," Karsh said, between gulps of air.

"Times change. People change. And therefore, old trickster, customs change." Ileana was sitting cross-legged under the tree, filing her nails while she waited for him.

"Some people," Karsh said, trying to laugh but

merely wheezing, "don't change. They just become more so. Take you, for instance —"

"Must we?"

"You were an outspoken child," the ancient tracker observed, "a rude adolescent, and you've become a most disrespectful adul —"

"All true. Too true." Ileana grinned insolently. "But I'm also a remarkable . . . goddess. Even Rhianna was impressed when I dropped Fredo on the Council's doorstep. They'd been trying to get him for years — as an accessory or accomplice to something or other — Her Majesty, the Potato, told me."

"Did Lady Rhianna explain his crime?"

"Better to ask, did I care? I was so eager to rid myself of that putrid package I just left him with her. Do all Thantos's underlings stink?"

"In a manner of speaking." Karsh grinned. "But I suspect that Fredo was being punished. For not capturing the girls at the hospital. I imagine he was quite surprised to see you there — though he thought that you were me."

"I told you my impersonation was brilliant! So what are you saying, that Thantos rolled Fredo in a dung heap because the big oaf had failed to snatch Cam and Alex?"

"So I suspect. It's been done before," Karsh said. "Let us hope the next one he sends will smell sweeter."

"The next?" Ileana questioned.

"And the next . . . until he traps them or we trap him. Now, put away that nail file, Ileana. You're on sacred ground."

"What, this old hill?" Ileana scrambled to her feet, tucked the file back into her herb pouch, and reached out to help Karsh up the last few steps.

"Thank you, dear girl," he said, leaning against the tall elm.

"Well, I wouldn't want you to perfume me with rotten eggs," she laughed. "Sit down. You're all out of breath. Surely an esteemed elder is allowed to rest even in a sacred place."

Karsh was stroking the tree as tenderly as if it were human. "Someday, I hope to rest here," he said, "with the spirits of my ancestors."

Ileana came toward the tree. Awestruck, she reached out, but stopped short of touching it. "Is this the one? I thought it was in Salem."

"Near enough," Karsh said sadly. "Many witches were hanged here in that time of fear and ignorance. My own great-grandmother was among them. She was a great healer. Today, she might have been a doctor. There were no women doctors then. There were only the gifted who opposed bloodletting and leeches and noxious tonics —"

"Do you remember her?" Ileana asked.

"I am not that old," Karsh protested. "But she comes to me in dreams now and then."

"I wish I knew my ancestors," Ileana pouted. "I don't even know my own parents. How old was I when you found me?"

She knew, of course, but Karsh told her again. "Three months or so. Just a bit older than the twins were when we took charge of them. Guess what your first word was?"

"You've told me. Over and over. My first word was *No.* You reached over to lift me from the meadow where I was hidden and I said, 'No.' Perhaps I meant it," Ileana mused sadly. "Perhaps it would have been better for me to stay there until whoever hid me returned."

It pained the old tracker to see Ileana so sad. He wished he could tell her everything. Who her parents were. And why it had been decided by the Unity Council that she should not know them.

Someday he'd tell her, Karsh vowed. And with that promise, he felt the tree grow warm beneath his hand.

He had felt its heat before. That time, the first time, he'd thought it was the morning sun warming the tree's crusty bark.

On this very hill, he'd waited, with an infant in his arms. He'd wondered whether he should remove her necklace, as Ileana — then a headstrong adolescent — had demanded. He'd wondered whether he'd chosen the right parents for the child. The right protector.

Karsh had met David Barnes at a conference for those curious about the ancient ways. The lawyer was interested and enthusiastic — but not a born warlock.

He had certain sensitivities. He could tell when evil was on its way — though not what it would look like. With enormous concentration, Dave could will a spoon to tremble, direct the movement of a Ouija board, and make a liar uncomfortable enough to want to tell the truth.

He was, as Dave himself put it, a sucker for innocence. He'd become a lawyer to do good in the world.

Still, Karsh had not been certain that David and his kind and patient wife, Emily, were the proper parents for such an exceptional child.

These thoughts had occupied Karsh's mind fifteen years ago, as he'd leaned against the tree waiting for Dave Barnes to appear.

And it was then that his great-grandmother had spoken to him for the first time outside a dream. The tree had became warm against his back. And her voice, strong and young — for she was only twenty-three when she'd been hanged — murmured words of reassurance to him.

Ye hath chosen well, son of my daughter's son. Safe shall thy fledgling be.

Ah, but had he made the right decision, had the Council chosen well, when they'd determined to keep Ileana's roots secret?

"Tell me!" the beautiful witch ordered suddenly. "I heard you, Karsh. I heard your thoughts. You know, don't you? You know who my parents are and will not tell me! You must. You must! It's not fair. Even the twins know the names of their parents —"

"Soon, Ileana," he said.

"Soon," the voice of his great-grandmother echoed. "Very soon."

Ileana heard the tree speak.

"Promise me, Karsh. Promise on this hallowed tree. On this, your great-grandmother's grave. On this sacred place where Camryn was given to her protector —"

"I promise," Karsh said. "Before I die, I will reveal to them their mother's fate — and to you, your father's name."

"Soon, you said," Ileana pressed him.

"Yes, child. Soon."

ABOUT THE AUTHORS

H.B. Gilmour is the author of numerous best-selling books for adults and young readers, including the *Clueless* movie novelization and series; *Pretty in Pink,* a University of Iowa Best Book for Young Readers; and *Godzilla,* a Nickelodeon Kids Choice nominee. She also cowrote the award-winning screenplay *Tag*.

H.B. lives in upstate New York with her husband, John Johann, and their misunderstood dog, Fred, one of the family's five pit bulls, three cats, two snakes (a boa constrictor and a python), and five extremely bright, animal-loving children.

Randi Reisfeld has written many best-sellers, such as the *Clueless* series (which she wrote with H.B.); the *Moesha* series; and biographies of Prince William, New Kids on the Block, and Hanson. Her Scholastic paperback *Got Issues Much?* was named an ALA Best Book for Reluctant Readers in 1999.

Randi has always been fascinated with the randomness of life. . . . About how any of our lives can simply "turn on a dime" and instantly (snap!) be forever changed. About the power each one of us has deep inside, if only we knew how to access it. About how any of us would react if, out of the blue, we came face-to-face with our exact double.

From those random fascinations, T*Witches was born.

Oh, and BTW: She has no twin (that she knows of) but an extremely cool family and cadre of bffs to whom she is totally devoted.

Go Interactive with your favorite T*WITCH!

Visit
www.scholastic.com/titles/twitches

It's Cam and Alex's very own website, and it's loaded with personal details they're dying to share. Visit their desktops, read their secret diaries, send them an e-mail and take the T*Witch Quiz! Also get a peek at what's next for these totally hip, mismatched twins.

And look for
T*WITCHES #3: SEEING IS DECEIVING
Since Alex arrived, Cam's best friend. Beth, feels like a third wheel. And matters only get worse when Beth rolls into the arms of the evil Thantos.

Available in bookstores this November!

SCHOLASTIC   TWW901